MW01228571

All characters in this book are fictitious,and any resemblance to actual persons living or dead is purely coincidental.

Cover photo by Al Hartman
Photo of Al Hartman Brittany Tamason

Copyright on 9-09-2020 by Al & Lorraine Hartman. All rights reserved. This book or any part may not be copied or reproduced without express permission of Al or Lorraine Hartman.

Special thanks to Janet Stout and
Lorraine Hartman

Books By Al Hartman

The Last Drive

Texas Bound

Drive The North Side

To Tame The West

Spitfire Mustang

Sulphur Springs Stranger

John Grigsby Witt

My Landing On Normandy

St. Elmo

The War Is Over ?

Vanished

Relentless

Western Passage

To Coach Allen

Marshal Maurice Allen knew they were near, but was having a hard time finding clear tracks, do to a hard rain that had just passed.

Suddenly............"OK marshal! Drop your guns!"

He was caught dead to rights.

Relentless 1

Maurice Allen was born a slave, in 1840, in the State of Missouri. In 1863 he heard of the, "Emancipation Proclamation." He had a fight with his Master and escaped.
Striking his Master was a criminal offense, and a warrant was issued for his arrest. He traveled, mostly at night, to Kansas. A state that's population was more anti slave than for slavery. Maurice worked for a blacksmith a couple of months, but got word he was being hunted, and people were asking questions.
He slipped out one night and headed south. He ended up in "Indian Territory," now the State of Oklahoma. Maurice was taken in by a tribe of Cherokee Indians, and learned their ways. He hunted with them and learned the art of tracking. He became a very good shot.
He learned the language of 5 different tribes, and got along well with most Indians. Occasionally a tribal war would break out, and he was regarded a warrior who knew no fear, and was decorated many times for his bravery. A lot of braves wanted no engagement with him. There was no fear in his soul.
At the end of the war Maurice Allen was officially a free man, and safe from prosecution. He staked a claim in Arkansas, and started a well laid out farm, with a few cows. He was a well built, strong man, a little over 6', wide shouldered and narrow at the hips.
His skill for tracking got around, and lawmen would hire him to hunt down criminals for them. None ever escaped

his hunt for them.

In 1875, the United States, wanted to tame the Indian Territory, and wanted to hire 200 Deputy Marshals. Maurice knew the territory so well, and his tracking abilities were great, so he was hired by a Federal Judge to be one of these needed men. This was unheard of. A Black Marshal? In the west?

Maurice Allen took the job. He bought a white horse, a black hat, shirt, pants and two Colt Peacemakers. He went to headquarters to pick up his first warrant. He was given the warrant for Willie Sparks. A mugger, a stage robber and bank robber. Sparks robbed a bank in Hampton Arkansas. Marshal Allen tucked the papers in his shirt and rode out.

He was joined by a Cherokee Indian known as "Lone Cat." Lone Cat was a very good tracker and a old friend of Maurice. They rode to Hampton and gathered information on Sparks. In the robbery Sparks shot the bank clerk, but it was not fatal. The arrest warrant was for bank robbery and attempted murder.

Willie Sparks had a career of trouble. From petty theft, stage holdup's, and several shootings. He was bad tempered and fast with his pistol.

Maurice walked around Hampton asking questions, and looking for any information that would be of help. He didn't get much. The best he got was which way Sparks headed, and some speculation of where he was heading. One cowhand that knew Sparks, and most likely had rode with him a time or two, gave the Marshal the most promising lead.

"If I was to look for him," the cowman said, "I'd poke around Fall River Bend in Kansas. It's not a town. Just a cluster of shacks hidden in a high rocky area. Hard to find, and hard to get to unnoticed."

Maurice gave him a silver dollar, thanked him and thought to himself, "Ain't no honor among thieves."

He and Lone Cat rode out of Hampton and started for Fall River. They had no hope of finding track, because it's been a few days, and wind or rain had most likely wiped them out. They rode until nearly dark and set up camp.

The next morning they ate a quick breakfast and headed out. Around noon, they stopped and made coffee near a clear stream. Two Indians approached them. Lone Cat spoke to them and asked if they wanted coffee. The two braves rode in. They were Shawnee.

Maurice asked them if they saw a white man heading this way, and gave them a rough idea what Sparks looked like. One of the braves told them a white man who matched that description, rode near them three days ago. He was riding a pinto horse.

That was good news to The marshal and Lone Cat. They were in luck. And they knew Sparks was riding a pinto. They finished their coffee and bid farewell to the Shawnee braves.

Again they rode until sunset and made camp. They were making good time, and it looked like they were on the mark. Fall River wasn't far away.

The next morning they had coffee and moved closer to Fall River. They saw some tracks occasionally, but they couldn't be sure they were Sparks. Could be any cowhand, as the trail was clear and open. Made travel easy.

As they got closer to the river, Lone Cat said softly; "I saw a rifle barrel flash."

"They mush have a lookout." Marshal Allen replied. "I'm gonna' put on my mask, make 'em think we're running."

Lone Cat nodded in agreement.

"Let's see if we can get him to acknowledge us." Maurice said, and waved his hand.

A man stood up from the rocks holding his rifle and shouted; "What-ya want?"

"Need a place to lay low!" The marshal replied.

"What ya running for?"

"Got a posse on our tail. Bout a day away."

"Cover yer' tracks an swing around behind these rocks," the lookout said, "you'll find a passage behind the cover of the brush."

Marshal Allen waved at the man and started around the rocks. Lone Cat followed, cleaning their tracks as he did. It took some looking to find the path as the brush had it covered well.

After clearing the passage, it opened up into a large clearing with a dozen makeshift small shacks. There was eight men standing there all with guns pointed at Maurice and Lone Cat.

"Who are ya' 'en what do you want?" One of the men asked.

"Lookin' to hide out for a couple of days," Maurice answered, "got a posse on our backs."

"Hope the hell you didn't lead 'em here." One of the men said. "We don't need the law down on us. Got enough trouble as it is."

"We covered our trail." Lone Cat said.

"Hope so," a man said, "sure do hope ya' did. Get down a spell."

Maurice and Lone Cat dismounted and took the saddles off their horses.

"Whats with the mask?" One of the men asked.

"Just habit. Feel naked without it." Maurice told him.

"Well you can be naked here."

Marshal Allen took the mask off.

"Lookie here boys, a blackie an a Injun. What a pair." All the men laughed.

"What ya running from, steal some liquor or candy?"

All the men laughed again.

Maurice and Lone Cat tied off their horses. Maurice asked; "Any off these sheds open?"

"The one with the half moon is." A man said, pointing to an outhouse. Again, the men with him laughed some slapping their leg.

Maurice walked to the man, grabbed him by the neck and lifted off the ground and said; "I've had enough for one day pal, now shut your face."

All the others had their guns pointing at Marshal Allen.

One of the men said; "Put 'em down."

"Go ahead and shoot." Maurice said as he held the man in front of him, holding a Colt in his left hand. "I'm asking for no trouble. Now put your guns away or fill him full of holes."

"OK boys," one of the men said, "fun's over, let 'em alone. They got trouble just as we do."

Some of the men grumbled and walked off. One of the men pointed at a shed across the way as he turned.

Marshal Allen and Lone Cat walked to the shed and put their saddles inside. There were two bunks, a table and a chair.

"Wonder which one is Sparks?" Maurice said.

"Maybe we'll find out tonight." Lone Cat said.

"Yeah most likely."

They laid a blanket on the bunks and took a rest. Both had a pistol laying next to them.

As it was coming to nightfall Maurice and Lone Cat went outside and washed up. They could smell a meal cooking form the larger shack in the center. They walked over and stepped inside. As they did it got quiet for an instant. As the men started back talking, one of the men pointed to chairs.

"Have a seat." He said. "Gonna be eatin' shortly. Have a seat."

They pulled out a chair and sat down. One man asked if they wanted a shot of whiskey. They both declined.

The meal was a deer steak and beans. It was done nicely, and tasty. The men talked, sometimes asking Maurice about his past. Maurice made up some story's about robbing stages and merchants. The men listened.

"You ever shoot anybody?" One asked.

"Here en' there," Maurice told them, "my friend here has shot more en' me though." Lone Cat gave him a look.

"Why are you here?" The marshal asked.

The men started telling their exploits, and one said; "Willie here's the newest," one man said, pointing to man next to him, "robbed a bank an shot the teller."

Maurice smiled and shook his head. He bumped his knee against Lone Cat's. He now knew his man.

Maurice and Lone Cat walked back to the shed they were staying in.

"Gotta find a way to get him alone." Maurice told Lone Cat.

"Ask him to help us recover our gold," Lone Cat replied, "tell him we hid it to travel faster. Tell him not to tell anyone and we will cut him in a share."

"Good idea Cat. Let me see if I can get him by himself." He patted Lone Cat on the back and went outside. Maurice saw Willie standing next the building they had dinner rolling a smoke.

"Psssst'." Maurice whispered.

Willie Sparks looked up. Maurice waved him his way. Willie walked over to him.

The marshal told Willie about the gold they had hidden, and if he would be willing to help. Willie smiled and said; "Be most willing to my friend. I like gold."

Maurice told him not to mention it to anyone. He figured once they got a few miles from the settlement, he and Lone Cat could overpower Willie and bring him back to Hampton. He told him to meet out from the rocky shelter in a hour.

Maurice and Lone Cat gathered their things, and snuck out to saddle their horses. They got the horses ready and eased out from the settlement.

They got a mile out and saw Willie waiting, and rode up to him.

"How far is it?" Willie asked.

"Should be there about noon." Maurice replied.

Willie shook his head; "Let's ride." He said, and gestured with his hand. He was thinking when they showed him where the gold was, he would shoot the two dummies, and take the gold for himself.

Marshal Allen had a deep feeling that Willie would want to do just that. He told Lone Cat to be on watch, and make sure Willie was always between them, so he would not have an advantage.

They rode into the night, and the marshal decided to make camp for the night. Willie Sparks protested; "Let's keep riding," he demanded, "never know if we ain't be-in followed."

"If you didn't tell anyone," Maurice answered, "we shunt have a problem."

"I dint say a thing to anybody!" Willie protested.

"Well good then, we shouldn't have ta' worry." The marshal told him. "We got all the time I the world to get rich."

Willie wasn't happy about the camp time, and it showed. That made Marshal Allen more sure of Willie's plan. He had a moment that he and Lone Cat could talk in confidence, and he warned him. Lone Cat told the marshal he had already figured that out too.

They slept through the night in peace. Only a coyote cry here and there.

The next morning Willie was up and had a fire going to make coffee.

16

"Get up boys," he called out, " gotta get that there gold men."

"We'll get the gold partner." Marshal Allen answered.

That made Willie Sparks jump as that answer was behind him, not the marshals bedroll.

"We'll have it by noontime." Lone Cat added from the opposite direction. That made Willie turn around again.

"Where you boys been?" Willie asked. "You been sneakin' the gold out?"

"No, we didn't get the gold," Maurice told Willie, "we never sleep in camp in case of Indian trouble."

"You mean I was alone here unprotected, all by myself?" Willie asked.

"No we had you covered," Lone Cat told him, "we were watching out for you Sparks."

Willie shook his head, and started making the coffee, and heating up some ham hocks he had brought with him.

After eating and finishing the coffee, they saddled up and rode eastward. They kept Willie between them so to have an eye on him. It got around noon time and Willie asked how much further. Maurice told him they were getting closer and not to worry.

The sun was beating down on them and the horses were getting sluggish. Marshal Allen suggested they take a break and give the horses some water. Lone cat rode up a rise to have a look around. He saw a small stream with some willows for shade about a half mile away. He waved and pointed. Maurice and Willie rode after him.

After they watered the horses, and filled their canteens,

17

Lone Cat started to make a fire.

"What' cha doing?" Willie asked.

"Gonna' make some coffee and fry some fish." Lone Cat replied. "Ain't ya hungry? I sure am."

"Hell no, I ain't hungry. I wanta' get to the gold. I'm beginning ta think you two are lying to me!"

"Well Mr. Sparks, we are." The Marshal said with both pistols in his hands. "Now put your hands up high. You're under arrest."

Willie Sparks turned to look at Maurice with anger in his eyes. "What's this all about?" He asked.

"I'm a U.S. Marshal, and you're being arrested for bank robbery and attempted murder in Hampton Arkansas. Lone Cat take his gun belt."

Lone Cat walked behind Willie to unbuckle his gun belt. When he reached to pull the strap, Willie poked Lone Cat hard to the stomach with his elbow, and turned to grab Lone Cat's gun. That's when Willie Sparks saw stars.

It was near dark when Maurice and Lone Cat rode into Hampton with Willie Sparks. They rode up to the sheriff's office. Sheriff Bailey came out to greet them.

"I see you got your man Marshal." He said.

"Yes sheriff we got him. It was a easy job. He gave us no real trouble."

"Well get 'em down, and I'll put him in the lock up."

Marshal Allen and Lone Cat helped Willie off his horse. Willie was grumbling in protest. They walked him in, and Sheriff Bailey locked him in his cell.

Marshal Allen signed the arrest warrant and gave it to the sheriff.

"Thank you Marshal," Sheriff Bailey said, "Here is your next warrant. It was sent here by telegraph just in case you brought in Willie Sparks."

Maurice took the paper and looked it over.

"Your the closest Marshal to this warrant at the time, so they sent it by chance."

Maurice looked it over. It was a warrant for three men wanted for a stage robbery in Arkansas and running to the Oklahoma Territory. They killed the driver and the guard, taking his shotgun. They got the strong box and all valuable items the passengers had. Oklahoma, known as Indian Territory, was a hot bed of murders, thieves, rustlers and the worst of the bad, hiding out there. A lot of lawmen wouldn't accept a warrant that went there.

Note;

Crossing into Oklahoma was called the dead line. Any lawman that entered there faced being killed, and by the time it became a state, 120 lawmen were murdered mostly by ambush. Outlaws would leave cards on trees or posts warning lawmen to stay out. Judge Parker demanded an end to this.

Maurice folded the note and stuffed it into his shirt pocket and told the sheriff he would be on his way.

"Hold up there Marshal Allen," Sheriff Bailey said, "got something for ya'." He opened his desk drawer and pulled out an envelope. "Here's your money!"

Maurice counted five hundred dollars and asked; "What's this for?"

"That's the reward money fella. They offered five hundred dollars for Willie Sparks capture. It's yours!"

Maurice was surprised. He didn't know he got the reward money. He thought he just got his forty dollars a month. It was a total surprise to him. He split it with Lone Cat. The sheriff shook his head and smiled. Lone Cat thanked Marshal Allen. He was surprised also.

Maurice asked the sheriff where the three men were last seen. The sheriff told him about three miles out of Big Oak, Arkansas, heading toward Oklahoma Territory, about five days ride from Hampton. Maurice went out to his horse to start the search. He thanked Lone Cat, and told him he would go alone on this one.

"Aren't you gonna' rest the night here?" Lone Cat asked.

"No I'll get some rest later tonight." Marshal Allen replied.

21

"Want to get some information as soon as I can."

Lone Cat shook Maurice's hand and told him to be careful. Maurice stepped into the saddle, and rode off.

He rode for several hours, and decided to make camp to let him and the horse some rest. He picketed the horse on some grass, and made some coffee. He had a ham hock left and heated it on a stick over his small fire.

After eating he rolled up in his blanket near some brush so as not to be seen easily. He drifted off to sleep.

About an hour before daylight, he stoked the fire to heat his coffee. He took the horse to the stream nearby to drink. A fish splashed startling the horse. He walked back to the fire, tied the horse to a bush , and walked back to the stream with a piece of string. He took a fishhook he had in his hatband, and tied the hook on. After scratching around in some leaf droppings, he found a grub, stuck it on his hook and tossed it into the stream.

It only took a minute to hook a nice brook trout. Maurice stuck a willow sprig into the trout to hold it over the fire. In a few minutes and the fish was ready to eat.

He ate his trout, drank one more cup of coffee, and then doused the fire. He saddled his horse and started for Big Oak, resting only short times to eat and nap.

Four days later, Marshal Allen rode into Big Oak as the town was just beginning to wake. Farmers and ranchers were coming in for supplies. There was man sweeping the boardwalk in front of Cobb's Whole Goods. He stopped and waved at Marshal Allen. Maurice waved back.

The marshal rode up to the sheriffs office, dismounted, tied his horse, and went to the door. When he grabbed the door knob he found the door was locked. He stepped back.

Walking to the window so he could look in, the window was shuttered. He walked back to the door and knocked. He heard nothing. He figured the sheriff hadn't come in yet. So he tried knocking again, just to make sure.

The marshal knocked harder and heard a voice call out; "Just hold your draws on a damn minute!"

Marshal Allen smiled and waited. He could see someone was peering through the peephole in the door.

The door swung open and the man was wear his long-johns and his boots'

"What's so damn important?" He asked. "It's only six thirty, and I had a late night with all the fights at the Big Oak Saloon last night."

"I'm U. S. Marshal Allen sir, I came to get some information on the stage robbery, and the killin', a couple of days ago."

"Your black. Ain't no black marshals!"

Maurice pulled back his coat, and showed his badge.

"Yes I'm black sheriff, and I am a U. S. marshal."

"How'd you get that badge? Steal it?"

Marshal Allen was get a little impatient. He reached into his pocket and pulled out the letter from the judge appointing him to be a marshal. He handed it to the sheriff.

The sheriff read the letter and shook his head saying;
"I'll be damned. I wouldn't have believed this if you told me."

"Well I told you , and you didn't believe it! Now can we get down to business?"

The sheriff motioned Maurice inside, saying; "I'll get some coffee going. Have a seat."

Maurice pulled out a chair, sat and asked: "Did you form a posse and go after them?"

"Sure did, but had to call it off."

"Why was that? Lose their trail?"

"No the trail was clear enough. That's why we stopped."

"I don't understand."

"They rode into Injun' territory..........Oklahoma!"

"But sheriff, I'm not sure why you would give up because of that?" Marshal Allen said. "Because of Indians?"

"No not Injuns. Every low life murderin' S.O.B. Runs to hide out there. Any lawmen that goe's there never returns. They even got signs posted waning lawmen they'll be shot."

"Looks to me,..... we need to clean that area up sheriff."

"You go right ahead my friend. Hope they at least bury ya'."

Marshal Allen asked if he could get some deputies.

"Ain't nobody gonna' volunteer. You're on your own pal."

Marshal Allen shook his head, and said goodbye to the sheriff, poured a cup of coffee, walked out and mounted his horse. He rode toward Oklahoma Territory sipping his coffee, and thinking.

The next evening he was at the border of Oklahoma Territory. He saw a sign tacked to a tree. It read; "Lawmen will be shot."

Maurice thought the sheriff was kidding about this. He took a deep breath, and rode on.

The problem was he had no trail to follow as the wind and weather cleared the ground. He saw a lot of fresh tracks, but they were not from the men he was after. A lot of the tracks were from Indian ponies, so he followed them to see if they could give him any information.

He was about to start looking for a place to camp for the night, when he smelled smoke. Marshal Allen followed the smell. In just a short ride he could see the smoke. He got down from his horse and tied it to a bush.

He decided it would be best to creep close to identify who was camping. He didn't want to come into a bunch of outlaws. That would be dangerous.

As he snuck closer to the camp a voice asked what he was doing, but the words were in Cheyenne. He turned and saw a Indian holding a rifle on him. Maurice told him, in the brave's language, he was a U.S. Marshal and was looking for three white murderers. The brave told him to get his horse and come into camp.

He walked into the camp. There was a small group of men, women and five youngsters. The Indian brave told the group who he was, and that he spoke their language. All the men greeted him, and the squaws tipped their heads as they held out a hand toward him.

Marshal Allen told the group who he was looking for and asked if any had seen the three men. The sheriff told Maurice one of the men was riding a palomino, and one was on a black horse with one white sock.

One of the older men told him he saw those two horses a day ago. They were camped roughly five or so miles from where they are now. He told Maurice when it became daylight he would show him how to find them.

"What a break," Maurice thought. He hadn't a clue, or any other idea where to look for these men. Nor did he have much to go on except the horses they were riding. This could save a lot of time.

The Indians cooked a meal, and Maurice made some coffee for them. They loved that. They ate a good meal of prairie hens and smoked fish. Maurice shared some salt. The Indians were very appreciated of the coffee and salt. Salt was hard to come by in the wide open, and so was coffee. They were very thankful.

Maurice was thinking, hopefully he could find the men before they moved. He had to be careful as there were so many outlaws in the territory, and they would kill him if they discovered out who he was.

The next morning after eating, the older brave had the marshal follow him to a rise outside of camp. He pointed to a high mesa several miles away. He told Maurice that the men were at the base of that mesa in a cluster of large boulders for protection. He also warned him they were well covered.

Maurice thanked him and returned to camp and saddled his horse. All the brave wished him luck and warned him of the danger of going alone. He thanked them for their concerns, and their hospitality, then mounted up . As he rode out of their camp they all waved. He rode very slow so not to stir any dust that could be seen for miles.

After an hour he was close to the mesa, and he smelled smoke and bacon. He figured they were cooking breakfast. He dismounted, tied his horse to bush. He could see the large boulders and eased closer. He heard no talking or any other noises. He knew he was taking a risk.

The lack of any noise made him worried. Did they see him coming?

Being next to a large boulder, he leaned forward to see if he could make out the camp site, he felt something push into his back!

"What you lookin' for?" A voice behind him asked.

Maurice stiffened and asked; "Can I turn around?"

"Sure, nice an slow, with your hands up."

He eased around and saw a man holding a double barreled shotgun with the hammers cocked. Most likely was carried by the guard on the stage. He had two men with him.

Maurice was sure he had his men, but they had him also.

29

"Was going to see if you could share some coffee."
Maurice said to the man.

"You a lawman?"

"No just a cow poke lookin' for work."

"Ain't no cows around here fella. You running from the law?"

Thinking quickly, Marshal Allen answered; "Had a mix up with some fellas back a piece. Had to get along, if you know what I mean."

"Ya I know what you mean. Eddie, check him over."

One of the men walked behind the marshal and started to pat him down. He then opened Maurice's coat exposing a bright silver star. The man backed up and nodded his head back at the marshal, and then at the man with the shot gun.

"Well, well," the man said, "don't look like you be tellin' the truth fella. Eddie, take his guns."

"Wait a minute," Maurice told the man, "I'm here to arrest you, so put down that gun, and surrender."

The man laughed; "Eddie get his guns an step back so you don't get hit from this scatter gun."

Eddie started toward the marshal.

"Hold it." Maurice said again, and took out a piece of paper and a pencil. "What's today's date?" He asked.

The man with the shotgun looked stunned, and said; "What difference does it make?"

"I have to have the correct date on the arrest papers."

That had the effect Maurice was hoping for . The man holding the shotgun glanced over his shoulder at Eddie, and the other man whose name was Lonnie Price.

30

When he did, Maurice grabbed the barrel of the shotgun just inches from his gut, and pulled it away from him. Eddie grabbed for his pistol, and the marshal fired a shot. It knocked Eddie over backwards at that short range.

"Now you two drop your gun belts before my friend behind gets nervous."

The man that was doing all the talking started to turn his head.

"I said drop you gun belts. Now!"

They both unbuckled and let them drop.

"Keep 'em covered Harry." Maurice called out.

"I got 'em." A voice replied.

Maurice looked behind the men and there was a tall well built black man holding a rifle standing there. Maurice nodded his head at him and said; "Preciate it friend, good timing."

"Heard some loud talking as I was riding by, thought I'd check it out Marshal. Glad I did, but with that double barrel in your gut I was hesitant to shoot."

The stranger walked up and picked up the two gun belts. He was well built, clean shaven, and a handsome man. Six feet tall, looked to be in his thirty's.

"Hi Marshal, my names is Isaac Taylor. Glad I could help."

"I'm glad you did, and not a moment too soon." Maurice told him. "My name is Maurice Allen, brother Taylor."

"Where you gotta' take 'em marshal?'

"Big Oak, Arkansas."

"I'll ride with ya' marshal. See to it you get them there."

"No need to do that Mr. Taylor."

"Ain't no problem marshal. I don't have anything going, and I'd feel better if you had some help. These two will kill you in a heartbeat if they get a chance. Call me Isaac."

"I appreciate your concern, Isaac, but don't want to interfere with your doings. You can call me Maurice."

"I got nothing doing right now. Just wandering from Texas, and somehow ended up in this God forsaken land."

"OK then Isaac, let,s get these two tied up an get ta' movin'."

They buried Eddie, then tied the two outlaw's hands together and started heading east. Riding until nearly dark they found a wooded spot near a stream. The water was clear and cool, and had some nice fish swimming in it.

They took a pair of handcuffs and connected the two prisoners together, made them sit at a sycamore tree, and wrapped a rope around them and the tree.

Maurice got his hook and string and walked to the stream.

Isaac started making a fire and some coffee.

After finding some grubs for bait, the marshal started fishing. It wasn't to long before he had four nice sized trout for making dinner. He grabbed some cat tails to make a cabbage like side to go with the fish.

The fire had some nice coals to cook the fish, and the coffee was ready. Isaac helped Maurice getting things ready. They put some willow branches across the coals, and laid the trout on them to roast. The cat tails were cut up, and put on the coals to boil.

Wasn't long before the meal was ready. They put two fish on a plate with the swamp cabbage, and gave it to the prisoners. They complained about having to eat with one hand. The marshal told them they were lucky enough he decided to feed them.

After eating, and cleaning the pot and plates, Maurice and Isaac had a coffee before going to sleep. Isaac told Maurice about his cattle work in Texas. He had worked for some big cattle drives that paid forty dollars a month. That was good money, but it was hard work too.

The average monthly pay for a working man was twenty five dollars.

Isaac told the Marshal Allen, he had saved some money and decided to have a look around the country a bit.

"Glad you did Isaac," Maurice said, "got to me just in time."

"You had things under control. All I did was back you up." Isaac told him.

"Well I'm glad you did Isaac. Hit the sack, I'll take the first three hours. Get some rest."

Isaac finished his coffee, and rolled up in his blanket. Maurice checked on the two prisoners tied to the tree, and tossed a blanket over them. He then eased back into the darkness, and set on a log. Knowing if you are a guard, you want to get out of the fire light.

He wasn't worrying about Indians, he was more cautious of what outlaws were out here. They had made a good camp site, the fire couldn't be seen at a distance. The air was cool, felt good.

He sat there looking at the stars and listening to the coyotes. Suddenly he heard a noise. Something was moving near him. He cocked the shotgun.

"It's OK friend," a voice said, "It's just me. Time for you to get some rest."

"Wasn't sure, what was tussling around camp." Maurice answered, and Isaac laughed.

The marshal eased off and got in his blanket. Felt good to get some rest.

The next two days went rather well. The two outlaw's were complaining about everything. Weather was nice. Cool in the mornings, and evenings, but quite warm during the day. The prisoners, Bert Woal and Lonnie Price, were bitching about the heat all day. Marshal Allen told them; "Better get used to it boys. You're gonna get plenty of it on the rock piles where your going!"

We ain't there yet, marshal," Bert said, "we'll just have to see about that."

That night after dinner, Lonnie said he had to relieve

himself. Isaac told Maurice he'd handle it, and unwrapped Bert and Lonnie's rope from around the tree.

"OK, let's go." Isaac ordered.

"Ain't ya' gonna leave him here?" Lonnie asked, nodding his head at Bert.

"Ain't no need for me to go," Bert added, "got no interest in being a part of that."

"Well don't watch." Marshal Allen shouted. "Go ahead Isaac,..........get it over with."

Isaac motioned for the two men to walk into the trees. When they got into the forest cover, they stopped quickly, and Isaac almost bumped into them. That's just what Bert was hoping for. Bert grabbed Isaac's arm and Lonnie grabbed for his gun. Isaac grabbed Lonnie's arm, and kneed Bert's gut. The two men wrapped their arms around Isaac, and squeezed him. All three were twisting around in a furious circle, but Isaac kept a hold on Lonnie's arm.

Bert butted Isaac's face with his head. It made Issac lose his grip on Lonnie's arm. Lonnie grabbed Isaac's pistol, and cocked it as he lifted it from the holster. Bert pushed Isaac back and hollered; "Shoot, shoot 'em."

There was a bang!

Marshal Allen stood there with his pistols drawn. Lonnie fell, pulling Bert down.

"Damn Marshal, glad you showed up." Isaac said. "I was a goner for sure. Thanks a heap."

"Glad I heard the ruckus, Isaac. I knew something was up. Unhook Lonnie, and put that cuff on Bert's other hand. I'll get a shovel. Keep an eye on Bert." Maurice went to get a shovel so Bert can bury his friend.

Bert dug Lonnie's grave, complaining all the way.

"Well, we only need to get him back now, Isaac, that'll save some food, and time."

Maurice cut a lock of Lonnie's hair before putting him the grave Bert dug. He also discovered Lonnie had a metal with his name on it around his neck. He took that too.

"That'll give us poof we had him. No sense losing the reward."

"Good idea." Isaac replied.

They covered the grave site, and rode for Big Oak.

It took two days to get to Big Oak, with Bert complaining and grumbling constantly. They rode straight to the sheriff,s office, and tied off their horses. They got Bert off his horse and went to the office door.

The sheriff met them at the door.

"Well looks like you at least got one of 'em." The sheriff said.

"No,........we got 'em all sheriff," Maurice told him, "but

had to bury two of 'em. Here's proof of the other two."

Marshal Allen showed the Sheriff, Lonnie's neck tag and hair, and a letter he found in Eddie's pocket that was addressed to Eddie.

"Well then Marshal, looks like case closed." The sheriff said. "Put him into the jail cell, and I'll get to workin' on your reward."

They put Bert into a cell. The sheriff told Maurice he may not have the money until in the morning.

Maurice asked about a place to get a meal, and a room for the night.

"That would be the Silver Bar Saloon." the sheriff replied. "Owned by Gloria Drummond, good food an' she might have a room or two left. She's a good ole lady, an don't take no ruff in' around."

Marshal Allen thanked the sheriff, and he and Isaac went out to find the Silver Bar. They didn't see it. Maurice asked a man sitting on a bench across the street.

"It's that a way friend." He told them, as he pointed. "Just outside a town a pace or so, just a short walk."

Marshal Allen thanked him, and he and Isaac walked down the street. When they got to last building on the street, they could see the lights of the saloon. They could hear the twang of a tinny piano playing.

As they walked inside everyone turned to look at them. The bartender wiped a spot at the bar for them, and asked; "Can I hip ya'?

Isaac laughed; "I haven't heard that in several years." He told Maurice. "After the war, I passed through a town in

Florida called Marianna. Folks there said hip ya, instead of can I help ya."

"You where in Marianna?" The barman asked.

"Yes I was," Isaac answered, "ever been there?"

"Yes. I lived there for years. What made you pass through there?"

"I was discharged from the army in Florida."

Note: Back in those days when you were discharged, you got paid, and found your way home the best you could.

"You one of the U.S. Colored Corp that helped tear up the town?"

"No, I joined up several years after the war." Isaac replied.

"It was a mess after they left." The bartender added. "Took all the cattle, all the horses, took our workers and even floated all the women cross the river, dropped 'em off an let the barges drift off. We had no help or horses to till our fields, and had to make rafts ourselves to get the women folk back."

"You mean they freed the slaves, don't you?" Isaac asked the barman.

"I prefer to call 'em workers."

Isaac just nodded his head.

"How about two bourbons?" Maurice asked.

The barman poured two drinks and asked; "Pushin' cattle?"

"No, I'm a U.S. Marshal, an my friend here, has been keeping me company."

"U.S Marshal! You're a Black man."

40

"That's obvious enough pal." Maurice replied.

"Ain't never heard of such a thing!" The bartender said.

Marshal Allen showed the barman his badge and added;
"Judge Parker swore me in himself."

"Well I'll be damned. I never thought such a thing would
ever happen. A black marshal."

"Does that bother you fella?"

"No......not a tall. Just never thought I'd see the day."

"And why not?" Isaac asked. "Because he's black.'

"Well I got nothing against, just never would have
figured."

"You don't think a black man is capable of being a
marshal?"

"Let's change the subject." The barman said filling the
glasses. "Have a drink on the house."

Isaac shook his head .

"Do you have any rooms?" Maurice asked.

"Got one left, an it's got two beds," the bartender replied,
"I'll get Miss Drummond for ya'."

As they were waiting, a man who appeared to have
Mexican blood came up to Maurice and shook his hand,
and said; "Congratulations my friend, and good luck."

Marshal Allen thanked him.

"Howdy men." A woman said as she walked toward
Maurice and Isaac. "I hear you need a room. I have one
left, and it'll be four dollars a night , two a piece."

"That will be fine ma'am," Maurice answered, "that will be
just fine. Most likely only will need it only for the night. I
get my reward money hopefully tomorrow."

41

"Reward!" The bartender said. "You brought in some bad guy?"

"As a matter of fact my friend, I brought in the men that robbed the stage. Only one alive though."

"Well that's doing something," the bartender said, "nobody here in town had the guts to go after them three thieving scoundrels. Sorry I acted such a fool."

"No problem friend." Maurice answered, and handed Miss Drummond four dollars.

"By the way Miss Drummond, what's the sheriff's name? I never asked, and he never said."

"Name's Furlin, Roger Furlin."

"He seems to be a little grumpy ma'am."

"Grumpy is right Marshal, but he has a reason to be. His wife has had enough of his putting his life on the line and she's moved to some place in New Jersey."

"That would make me grumpy too ma'am."

"Well last I heard Marshal, he's a gonna go get her, an drag her back."

"Wish him luck ma'am."

"Me too Marshal, me too."

Maurice and Isaac sat at a table to have some dinner.

Several of the cowmen in the saloon were talking about the Black Marshal, and both of them could hear it. So Isaac asked; "Did any of you go after the stage robbers?'

Some of them answered they did.

"So why didn't you get them?"

"We weren't about to get kilt in Indian Territory. He's a braver man than any of us. That's fer sure."

"I thank you gentlemen, just doing what I get paid to do."
Maurice told them.

Maurice and Isaac finished their meal and went to their
room.

It was a clean room with two beds. Marshal Allen pulled
his boots, and laid back on the bed. It felt good.

Isaac rolled a smoke and sat by the window watching the
street below. When finished, he had a drink of water, and
crawled into his bed. They were both snoring in no time.

Marshal Allen and Isaac, woke at day break, washed up, and went down stairs.

Miss Gloria Drummond was seating customers.

"Sleep well you two?"

"Yes ma'am we did," Isaac answered, "slept like a rock."

"A noisy rock." Maurice added.

"Don't you talk Marshal," Isaac replied, "You rattled the windows from time to time."

Miss Drummond laughed; "You gentlemen want to have breakfast?"

"Yes we do ma'am," Maurice answered, "everyone says it's the best in town, so I hear."

"Well I don't know 'bout that marshal, but my cook Willie is a real good cook. Have a seat over at that table close to the bar, and I'll take your order." Miss Drummond knew they would want to face the door.

Maurice and Isaac had eggs, ham and biscuits with fresh butter. It was a good breakfast. Maurice paid Miss Drummond, and thanked her for the room and the good meals.

"You gentlemen hurry back. You're welcome anytime."

They both thanked her again, and walked out the front door. As they walked into town, it was getting busy in Big Oak. Farmers coming in for supplies. Cowhands coming in to pick a thing or two, and ladies doing some shopping.

It didn't look like the sheriff was in his office yet. So they decided to have a look around town.

A young boy walked up to them, and said; "You are really U.S. Marshals?"

"I am," Maurice answered, "and he is a friend of mine."

"Well mister, you're the talk of the town." The young boy said. "Everybody is talking about you two catching those stage robbers. I'm mighty proud to meet you."

"Thank you young man," Maurice said, "and it's nice to meet you young man." He reached in his pocket and handed the boy a two-bits silver coin. The boy looked at the coin, his eyes as big as goose eggs.

"Wow, …..thanks sir. I never had a quarter dollar before."

Maurice patted the boy on the head. The youngster ran off calling to his mother in excitement. Isaac smiled.

They stopped in a store to look at the goods for sale. Isaac bought a nice red shirt, and Maurice bought a pair of cotton socks.

As they stepped outside, a voice called out; "Hey you."

The marshal and Isaac turned and saw a man, in his late twenties early thirties, standing in the street.

Maurice pointed to himself, as to question, me?

"Yeah you." The man said. "Did you kill Lonnie Price?"

"Well, I had to friend. He was going to kill my friend here."

"You killed Eddie Blake too!"

"Well, ….yes, I had too." Marshal Allen replied, " he was going to kill one or us for sure."

"Lonnie was my brother," the stranger said, "an I'm going to even the score. Now draw!"

"I've got no quarrel with you my friend." Marshal Allen

told the man.

"You do now. Pull your iron!"

"Do you realize he's a U.S. Marshal?" Isaac asked.

"Don't much care who he is. He killed me brother."

"It was in self defense," Isaac replied, "you'll hang for it."

The stranger reached for his gun, and so did Maurice and Isaac.

"Hold it men, I got this." It was Sheriff Furlin stepping from an alley with his gun in hand. "Now give me your gun Willard." He said, and held out his hand.

"I can't let him get away with this." Willard said. "He killed my brother."

"Look Willard. You are all your Mom has left." Sheriff Furlin told him. "Your paw and your two brothers are dead from gun violence, and you are all she has to support her. You want to let her try to survive on her own?"

Willard handed his gun to the sheriff.

"Now you go home Willard, and you'll get your gun back when these two men leave town. Now git!"

Willard walked to his horse and rode out of town.

Maurice and Isaac walked to sheriff Furlin; "Thanks sheriff," Isaac said, "was lookin' tense there for a minute or so."

"No problem boys, I mean men. Sorry about that."

"Back east sheriff, everybody call's everybody boy, black or white." Isaac said. "Most of the south it gets touchy. Personally I don't give a damn. Guess I'm used to it from back east."

They walked to the sheriff's office, and Roger started

making coffee.

"Have a seat men. Coffee It'll be ready in no time. No point makin' it at home. Just sit there an drink it myself. Might as well do it here."

"Miss Drummond said you and the wife had a fallen out." Marshal Allen said.

"Fallin' out? She moved out!"

"That's what we heard sheriff."

"Don't know why shes gotta be a tellin' everybody."

"I guess it was my fault sheriff," Maurice replied, "I was askin' about your attitude."

"Attitude?"

"Well I asked her why you were so grumpy, and she told us about your wife leaving."

"Grumpy? She needs to mind her own business. I'm sorry to be that way. Got a lot on my mind."

"I'm sure you do." The Marshal answered.

"Been up holding the law since I was twenty years old. Got tired of pushin' cows and kissing the bosses butt. That's all I know. Keeping the law."

"I guess she wanted you to retire." Isaac added.

"And do what? Sit on my butt or scratch out a living. She got in a huff an pulled out. Last I heard she's in New Jersey."

"You going there to get her?" Maurice asked.

"Yep, sure am. Gonna drag her back here where she belongs, just as so as I can get you takin' care of."

Isaac raised his eyebrows.

The pot was boiling, so the sheriff started filling cups. It turned out hot and strong. Sheriff Roger Furlin sat at his desk, and said; "Waitin' on the banker. Should be here anytime now."

They all sat there not saying much. A stage pulled in, and started unloading. The street was busy with people coming and going. A man came to the door.

"Sheriff got a telly this morning." It was the banker. "Might want to read this." He handed it to Sheriff Furlin.

Sheriff Furlin read the telegram, and shook his head as he dropped it on the desk.

"Well Marshal,.....looks like we got a problem."

"What's that?" Maurice asked.

"Seems the U.S. Marshal's office says the stage company owes you the reward. Not them."

"Didn't the Marshals office send the order to arrest those men?" Marshal Allen asked.

"Yup,....sure did." Roger replied. "Got a copy right here. Looks like you and I are gonna have to hang around a while till they get this figured out."

"That's not a problem," Maurice said, "don't mind loungin' a bit."

"I was a hopin' ta' be headin' east an get my woman back here." Roger said.

"That may be a chore." Isaac added. "Sounds like she's made up her mind."

"Well she better un-make it, cause I ain't gonna' die being a farmer."

"The problem is, she doesn't want you to die being a sheriff." Maurice told Roger. "She doesn't want to see you all shot up."

"Ain't happened yet Marshal!"

"No not yet, and hopefully it never will," Maurice replied, "but you have to understand, your wife is in fear of it, and she doesn't want to witness it."

"Yea I know. I hope I can change her mind. I'll get the town to hire a deputy to back me up. Maybe that will calm her down."

"Maybe so Sheriff, I hope, maybe so."

Marshall Allen, and Isaac Taylor, walked their horses to the edge of town to the Silver Bar Saloon. They went in and told Miss Drummond they were going to be a day or so waiting to be paid. She told them that would not be a problem, and gave Marshall Allen the key to the room.

"Take as long as you need Marshall," she said, "glad to be of service."

Maurice and Isaac thanked her, and decided to take a ride in the country.

There were wooded plots scattered all along the large fields of grass. In the background were old and new growth mountains. In one spot they saw antelope and deer.

Marshal Allen was thinking about Willard Price. It worried him that Willard's mother lost all her family to gun fire. Willard was all she had left, and he needed to step up an take care of her.

Then his thoughts came to Miss Drummond. How did she get out here and how did she get started in the saloon business?

Then he thought of Sheriff Roger Furlin. What was he gonna' do, or have to do, to get back with his wife?

"You're quiet Maurice," Isaac said, "What ya thinkin"?"

"Isaac, when I get out in open country like this, my mind wonders from one thing to another. Old habit I've had. Besides, being alone as much as I am, it keeps me from going loony."

"I talk to myself, or to my horse," Isaac told Maurice, "the

horse doesn't say anything, but seems to listen well."
Maurice smiled.

"Look there." Maurice said, pointing his finger at the ground. "Horse tracks."

"Looks like Indian ponies." Isaac added.

"Sure does Isaac, wonder who they are."

"I hope they are friendly Marshal."

"Me too!"

They rode on keeping their eyes open. Marshal Allen pulled up his horse.

"What's up Marshal?"

"A buffalo track. Don't see many of them around here now days. Gotta' go up in the Dakota's to see 'em now, and the herds are not as big as they once were."

"Yeah, they hunted them hard." Isaac replied.

They came to stream. Maurice could see several trout swimming among the rocks.

"Let's catch some lunch Isaac. You like trout?"

"I sure do my friend. Good and tasty fish."

Maurice got down from his horse and got his hook and string.

"Isaac, dig around, and see if you can find some grubs. I'll find me a sapling to make a fishing pole."

He found a slender elm, and cut it off. He trimed it, and tied his string to it. Isaac had several grubs and a couple of crickets in his hat.

It was no time at all, and they had three rainbows and a brook trout, all about fourteen inches in length.

They made a fire, and put the trout on some willow

branches to cook. They also had water going for making coffee. Maurice and Isaac put the fish on a tin plate to cool while the coffee was brewing.

They were in a hollow and Maurice saw the sunlight dim from behind them.

"Isaac," he said, "there is someone behind us. When you turn, have your gun in hand. Careful."

They both turned at the same time, gun in hand. There was two Indian braves standing there with rifles. The braves held up a arm, hand flat. One of the braves said in Shawnee; "We in peace."

"Come in, eat." Maurice said in their language. The braves nodded their heads, and walk to the fire. One of the braves said they smelled the fish and coffee, and had to check it out. Maurice held out the plate, and each brave took a fish.

Isaac poured coffee in cups. The fish were gone in an instant. Marshal Allen took his pole to the stream. The braves never saw a fishing pole before and were amazed how it worked. Maurice had four more fish in no time and put them on the fire.

These were probably the Indians that left tracks further back. The braves told them they were with a small hunting party, and had set up a camp further down stream.

After eating they talked for a while. The braves thanked Maurice and Isaac for the meal and coffee. Maurice went to his saddle bag and got a fish hook and a piece of string. He gave it to the braves, and showed them how to use it. They were really excited, and couldn't wait to show the others back at their camp how well it worked. The braves mounted up, said goodbye, and rode off.

"You speak their language well Maurice."

"I've lived a good while with Indians Isaac. I speak several of their languages."

"Glad you do. At first I thought we were in a tight."

They rode for a while longer, then headed back to Big Oak.

They rode to Miss Drummond's Silver Bar Saloon, tied off
their horses. There was a young boy sitting on the sidewalk.
"Young man," Maurice said, "will you take these two
horses to the livery stable for me?"
"Yes sir I will." The boy replied.
Marshal Allen gave him two-bits, and said; "Thank you
young fella. Ask the man to give 'em some oats too."
The boy looked at the silver coin, and back at Maurice
with a smile on his face, saying; "Sure will sir, I sure will!"
He led the horses into town. Maurice and Isaac stepped
inside the saloon. They were met by Miss Drummond.
"Howdy men, have a good day?"
"Yes ma'am we did." Marshal Allen answered. "Ready for
a hot bath and one of your good meals."
"Well I'll get that bath a workin' for ya', an here's
something for you from Sheriff Furlin." She handed
Maurice an envelope.
He opened it, and found six hundred dollars, a note and a
telegraph. The note said;

Marshal here is the reward money from the stage line.
They had a two hundred bounty on those men dead or alive.
The telegraph is from the U.S. Marshals office. Hope you
do well, and be as safe as you can.
I'm a headin' East, hope to see you again.

Maurice handed it to Isaac to read.

The telegraph said;

Here are your orders to head to Dallas Texas to help the
Texas Rangers. Stop
They are wanting to capture Bryan Joiner. Stop
He is wanted for several warrants. Stop
He is considered dangerous. Stop
Good Luck Roger. Stop

Maurice let Isaac read that too.
"Looks like you got a new job to do Marshal." Isaac said.
"Looks that way my friend. You wanta go?"
"Well I'm lookin' for work,.........I'll ride to Texas with you.
Might find a job there."
Maurice counted the money, and gave Isaac three hundred
dollars.
"Oh no Marshal, that's too much for what little I did." He
handed Maurice two hundred back. Maurice wouldn't take
it so Isaac stuffed the money in Maurice's coat pocket.
"Isaac you saved my life!"
"And you saved mine friend. Keep your money for your
family."
Miss Drummond told them their bath water was ready.
"Thank you ma'am. We are gonna' get some fresh clothes.
Be right back."
They got fresh clothes, and went to the bath house. The
water was hot, and it felt good. They both lit a thin cigar,
and relaxed in the hot water. It was nice.
After getting into their fresh clothes they went to a table

and gave Miss Drummond their order.

They had a buffalo steak, mashed potatoes cabbage topped with bacon.

As they were eating, five cowhands came into the saloon. They went to the bar and ordered whiskey. They appeared to have had a head start drinking before they came in.

One of the men turned and faced Maurice and Isaac.

"You boys needed some work?"

"No we're movin' out in the morning." Maurice told him.

"I suggest you change your mind. I got a lot of cattle to move an need some help."

By this time the other four men had turned and were looking.

"Well I'm sorry friend but I already have a job to do." Marshal Allen replied.

"Maybe you didn't hear me to well fella." The cowman said. "I need men, and I don't care who. Now finish your meal and get ready to move out."

"Maybe you didn't hear what the man said," Isaac told the cowman, "now have your drink and you get out!"

"Don't you talk to me like that blackie, you better get ta' pullin' some iron boys. I've had enough."

"And so have I pal," Frank the bar man said holding a shotgun, "now finish your drink, and get ta' hell outta' here!"

The five cowhands didn't like looking down the barrel of that shot gun. They backed up.

"You men got a choice." Maurice said. "If you don't do as the man asked, ain't no cattle going anywhere, cause you'll be in jail." Marshal Allen pulled his vest open and showed his badge. The five men were shocked when they saw it.

"You heard the marshal," Frank said, and pointed the gun barrels at the door. "Now git."

The man, who had been doing all the talking, threw silver coins on the bar and all five men scrambled for the door.

"Thanks Frank." Maurice said. "Thanks a lot."

"No problem marshal. I didn't want ta' mop the floor again." Isaac and Maurice laughed.

They finished their dinner and retired to their room.

The next morning, they finished their breakfast and said goodbye to Miss Drummond.

As they got to the door, Miss Drummond called: "Marshal!"

As Isaac and Maurice turned to her, the door was shattered by bullets from gun fire in the street. It was a good thing they turned or they would have been gunned down.

They both drew their guns and eased to look out the door. Bullets sprayed around them again. It was the five cowhands that had been on the Silver Bar Saloon the night before.

Maurice told Isaac; "Let's go around from the back door."

They went to the back and slipped outside. They split up and each went to the front from each side of the saloon. That caught the cowmen by surprise. Maurice and Isaac stepped out firing. Two of the men went down and another was hit. The remaining men ran for cover behind a wagon.

Both sides exchanged shots for a couple of minutes. Maurice and Isaac were flat against the sides of the saloon. Frank the barman fired a shot out the front door with his shotgun. It shattered a wheel on the wagon and knocked the wounded man down. He moved no more.

Some of the cowhands in town came running up the road, rifles in hand.

"Throw your guns down and come out," Maurice hollered, "with your hands up."

The two remaining men stepped out.

By that time the cowmen from town were on them.

"Take them to the sheriff's office, and lock them up until you can get can a lawman and judge to hold a trial." Maurice told the men.

He walked to the men that came to help them, and picked out two of the hardest looking in the group. "I deputize you two to keep watch over these two men until help arrives. Tell them I arrested them for attempted murder of a U.S. Marshal and a U.S. Citizen."

The men agreed and removed the two cowhands back to town with a rope around their necks.

"Thanks again Isaac. Thanks for your help."

"Glad to be of service Marshal. Glad I could help you. Was a good thing Miss Drummond called for you!"

"Ya, I wonder what she wanted?"

They walked back to the saloon. Frank was standing there with his shotgun. He said; "That sure was an ambush, marshal. Had to stand with ya."

"Thanks Frank. I needed all the help I could get. That was a stupid idea they had."

"Yes it was marshal. Really dumb."

Miss Drummond came from the bar.

"What did you want to see me about ma'am?"

"I just wanted to tell you goodbye again and tell you to come back anytime!"

Maurice looked at Isaac, and they both laughed.

"Thank you ma'am, you saved our lives." Maurice said. "Hope to see you again."

Frank poured two drinks; "A parting salute gents. On the

house."

Maurice and Isaac drank the shots and waved goodbye as they walked out. They paused at the door this time.

Maurice and Isaac walked into town, got their horses, and rode out.

It was a nice day, not too hot, and a nice breeze.

The weather continued to be very nice, not too hot or too cold. It would take about a week to get to Dallas, if all went well. They rode until it was past mid day, and stopped, to have some coffee and a quick meal.

Marshal Allen got out the coffee pot, and found some smoke cured ham that Miss Drummond had slipped into his saddle bags. He thought that was so nice of her to do.

Isaac had the fire going in no time, and Maurice put pickets on the horses so they could eat some grass. Coffee was ready in no time at all, and the ham was warmed up. They sat and enjoyed their lunch.

As they were finishing, Isaac grabbed his rifle and fired a shot. Maurice grabbed for his. When traveling strange country it was always good to have your rifle handy.

"What is it? Where is it?" Maurice asked, looking hard for something to see.

"Turkey my friend. We will eat well tonight!" Isaac answered.

"Pugh partner, you damn near scared my britches off!"

"Sorry, I couldn't say anything, or he would have scooted." Isaac told him. "He was about to see us. Had to let fire."

Maurice just grinned, and shook his head.

Isaac got up and went into the bushes. He came back with the turkey.

They broke camp and started on. Isaac had the turkey across his saddle so he could pluck it.

As the afternoon passed, and it was coming to the the end

of the day, the air had became cooler. The cotton wood and junipers were getting thicker as they were leaving the plains. The hills became larger. It wouldn't be but a few days and mountains would appear in the distance.

As evening began to fall they found a nice clear stream and decided to make camp. They unsaddled the horses and wiped them down with some grass, and picketed them to eat grass.

Isaac had the fire going with the turkey on a rough made spit to turn it. Maurice went to the stream and cut some cat tails to make a cabbage like side dish. Isaac was looking through his saddlebags and found a paper bag. It had several muffins Miss Drummond had made. That would touch off dinner. He made a grill from some willow branches and warmed them up. He wished he had some butter to spread on the muffins, so he smeared some bacon grease on them.

After an hour or so some of the turkey was done. They carved up the turkey, and had a nice meal ready. The cat tail cabbage was cooked with a ham hock that added a good flavor. They let the rest of the turkey cook as they ate and had their fill.

After cleaning up the dishes, they sat by the fire and sipped coffee. Isaac had salted down the remaining turkey to help preserve it, and hung it in a tree to keep critters from it. It would make a couple more meals.

Isaac rolled a smoke and Maurice was gathering straw to make beds. Isaac heard something moving in the darkness. "Psst." He whispered.

Maurice turned to look at him.

Isaac pointed to his ear, and then in the direction the noise came from. Maurice grabbed his rifle.

"Hey there!" A voice called out. "OK to come in?"

"Ride in friend," Isaac answered, "nice and easy."

The rider came in and pulled up. "Glad I saw the fire," he said, "got too dark to see anymore turkey feathers."

Maurice and Isaac got a tickle out of that.

The rider got down and Maurice asked him if he wanted a cup of coffee.

"Sure would be nice," he said, "I used the last of mine this mornin'. Let me dig out my cup."

Isaac and the marshal watched carefully, just in case. The man walked to the fire and poured a cup.

"Boy that's good." He said as he sipped it.

"Where ya headin'?" Isaac asked.

"Ridin' down to Dallas. Got some business to take care of."

"That's where we are a headin'." Isaac replied.

"Mind if I travel with ya'," the stranger asked, "feel like it would be safer with Injuns about."

"Have you seen any?" The marshal asked.

"No, but I've seen a lot of sign. Mostly headin' north in bunches of ten to twenty. Might be hunting party's or maybe a raid on other tribes. Not sure, but they could be a huntin' targets of opportunity like you and me!"

"Has there been any trouble?" Isaac asked.

"Not so far, but you never know."

The stranger took another sip and said; "Names Jim, Jim

Glass."

"I'm Marshal Allen, and this is a friend, Isaac Taylor."

"Nice to meet ya'll." Jim replied.

Maurice nodded his head at Isaac, and Isaac did the same, which meant the man seemed OK.

"Want something to eat?" The marshal asked.

"No I'm fine," Jim answered, "ate a parcel of apples following those turkey feathers. Wasn't sure who made them, but happy it was you two. Didn't know if it was Injuns. Not sure how that would have turned out."

The three men sat and talked for a while before hitting the blankets. It wasn't long before they were all snoring in unison.

Shortly before daybreak, Maurice heard some rustling outside of camp. He reached over and nudged Isaac. Isaac rolled over, rifle in hand. Then a man walked into camp. It was Jim.

He had gathered some twigs and had the coffee pot filled with water. Isaac and Maurice took a sigh of relief. Jim had the fire going quickly. Maurice had added coffee to the pot and put it on the fire.

Jim laid several eggs next to the fire. He had found quite a few duck nests, so he took just one egg from each. Looked like eggs and ham for breakfast.

Marshal Allen was getting ready to cook when he looked up and saw ten Indians on horses staring at him. He alerted Jim and Isaac, and told them not to panic just yet, and grab for any guns.

The braves were in full war paint with rifles across their laps. One of the braves said something. Maurice knew then they were Shawnee. He answered in their language and invited them into camp.. That surprised the braves.

"Better make some more coffee," Maurice said, "they must have smelled it."

The braves tied their horses and walked to the fire. The one who appeared to be the leader, pointed to the coffee pot, and asked if it was coffee. Marshal Allen told it was and handed him a cup. The brave pointed to the others with his hand circling. Maurice told him they were making more. The brave shook his head. He sipped the coffee and said;

"Good coffee!" in his words. Maurice told him thank you!

The brave then asked Maurice, how did he learn his language?

Maurice told him of his life living with the Shawnee, Sioux, Cherokee and others. He told him he learned to hunt, fight and survive as he was with them. He also told the brave he fought in their battles with hostile tribes. Isaac could tell the warrior was impressed with Maurice.

Isaac started pouring coffee to the other braves. They really liked coffee and just gulped it down quickly.

Maurice asked the brave if they were going to a fight? The brave told him they were going to a meeting with the Sioux, and other tribes at the Little Bighorn River in Montana territory. He said there were problems with whites trespassing onto the Crow Reservation and they were going to see if they could have it stopped by the big chief in Washington.

"I hope you can get it done without harm," Marshal Allen said, "the Big Chief wants to work with his Indian brothers."

The brave shook the Marshals hand, and told him he was in hope.

The braves thanked Isaac, Jim and Maurice for the coffee, returned to their horses and rode off.

The three men finished their breakfast, and continued for Dallas.

Note: On June 26, 1876, just 3 weeks after the meeting with the braves, General Custer's entire force was annihilated at the Battle of the Little Big Horn.

The trail to Dallas was about two days to go. Maurice would be glad when they got there. It was a long ride. He was wondering why the Rangers wanted him to help. It seemed to him they should have plenty of good men.
Finally, as they rode into Dallas, it was midday and the streets were busy. Wagons were coming and going. Ladies were shopping, cattlemen riding in and out. Marshal Allen asked a man on the street where the sheriff's office was. The man pointed down the street, waved and walked on.
Isaac rode with Maurice, and Jim Bass said; "Hope to meet ya again Marshal. Nice ridin' with ya." Maurice tipped his hat to him, and Isaac waved.
They rode to the sheriff's office, got down and tied the horses off. They then walked into the sheriff's office, and both took their hats off as they did.
"Howdy!" A man behind the desk said. "What can I do for you?"
"I'm Marshal Allen, and this is a friend Isaac Taylor. I was asked to come here to meet with some Texas Rangers."
"Marshal Allen it is." The man said as he reached out his hand. "I've heard a lot about you in the last two weeks. I'm Sheriff Bert Davis. Have seat."
Marshal Allen and Isaac pulled up chairs.
"Let me send for the head Ranger. He's at the hotel just down the street." Bert told them, and he walked to the door. He called a boy on the sidewalk, and asked him to get the ranger. He sat behind his deck, and asked; "How was your

73

trip to Dallas?"

"Was a long ride, but went well." Maurice answered. "No trouble at all. Met some Indians, and they were friendly."

"Heard there were several large groups a headin' north." The sheriff replied. "Not sure why though."

Marshal Allen told the sheriff what the braves told him about a meeting with the Sioux over whites trespassing.

"I've heard they found large deposits of gold on Sioux land." Sheriff Davis said. "Heard it's causing trouble."

"Hopefully they can get the U.S. Cav to run 'em out." Maurice told the sheriff.

A tall strong looking man, around mid-forties, stepped into the sheriffs office. He held out his hand to Maurice; "I'm Will Barrett, Texas Ranger, good to see you!"

Maurice stood and shook his hand, and said; "Good to meet you Ranger Barrett. This is my friend Isaac Taylor." Ranger Barrett shook Isaac's hand also.

"Marshal, I've asked you here to help us catch Bryan Joiner. He's a tough one to corral. He is handy with a gun. Can disappear in a second. He is woods wise, and can cover his trail. I met a man that told me you could find him because you are so much like him."

"Well Ranger Barrett, I can track well, but I can't promise I'll find him."

"From what I've heard Marshal, you'll find him."

"I'll do my best sir. Tell me what you can."

Isaac told Maurice he was going to move on to look for work. He asked the ranger if there were any ranchers looking for help. Ranger Barrett told him where the Dallas cattlemen met, and suggested he check there. Isaac shook Marshal Allen's hand, and told him he enjoyed the time with him, and left the room.

"You take care my friend," Maurice said, "see ya' again."

Ranger Barrett sat with Maurice at a table, and started telling him about Bryan Joiner.

Bryan was 35 years of age. His lifestyle was a lot like Marshal Allen's. He too had lived with several Indian tribes, and spoke their language. He was atoned to the wild lands of the west. He was a good tracker and could survive off the land. He is a very good shot, and a master of ambush.

Ranger Barrett told Maurice where Bryan Joiner was last seen. He was wanted for murdering a popular cattleman when caught rustling some of his cows.

"Well there you have it Marshal. Right now I can only spare two or three men to help you. Things are tight at the moment. Be alert, and watch your back."

"I thank you Ranger Barrett," Maurice answered, "but I rather would like to work this alone. Less chance of something going a foul. Do you have a description of his horse?"

"Yes, it is a good sized dapple gray. And here is a hand drawn likeness of Bryan Joiner. Everyone says it's pretty accurately done. Good luck!"

Maurice took the picture and put it in his shirt pocket. He and the Ranger shook hands, and the Marshal went out, mounted his horse. He rode down to the livery stable.

A man came out to meet him.

"Can I help ya'?' The man asked.

"I would like to leave my horse here for a few days." Maurice told him. "Not really sure how long. I want to rent a good mountain horse, dark in color if you have one."

The marshal didn't want to ride his big white horse after Bryan Joiner, just in case Joiner had been tipped off.

"You're in luck fella." The stableman answered. "Got a big black one with sure enough feet. Take ya' on a good mountain ride. Belonged to a trapper."

"That will be fine my friend," Maurice replied, "I'll switch out my tack. Why did the trapper get rid of him?"

"He didn't. The horse killed him."

"Oh great!" Maurice said.

"Can ya' ride?" The stableman asked.

"Well sure, but!"

"No need ta' worry. If ya understand horses you'll be OK. I'll give ya a tip. If he starts to wiggle his ears back an forth, he's seen or smelled something he don't like, or he's thinking about unloadin' ya'."

Maurice's eyebrows went up and down. He thought; Damn horse is as unpredictable as Bryan Joiner.

The man went to get the horse and the marshal started taking his saddle and gear from the big white.

The stableman brought out the big black. He was all muscle too!

After swapping his gear, Maurice gave the man twenty five dollars.

"You gonna be gone for months?" The man asked.

"I hope not, but want to make sure you're covered."

"Well OK then pal, I'm covered."

Marshal Allen went to put his foot in the stirrup, and the man said; "Gotta tell ya' friend, that horse can be a little surly at times, so keep your seat!"

"Will do, thanks." Maurice said as he swung onto the saddle, and started off.

The ranger had given Maurice a map to where Bryan was last seen. He rode in that direction.

As he was riding he saw a large cattle drive heading north. One of the cowboys started riding toward him.

"Hey partner," the cowhand hollered, "got me a job!"

It was Isaac Taylor. "Twenty five a month working for the

Lassiter ranch!'

"Good for you pal. Good for you. Where you headin'?"

"They said the railroad built a cattle pen three hundred miles from here an we are moving these doggies there."

"You be careful pal," Maurice told him, "and good luck."

"Will do Marshal, will do. Good luck to you also."

Maurice waved at Isaac, and rode off. He was glad Isaac found work.

 Marshal Allen had a good ride to the ranch, where the cattleman had lived, to ask questions about his murder. It was a full days ride and he got there as it was getting close to darkness. He was delighted the horse hadn't caused any trouble.

 He rode into the yard, and up the the house. A man came out to greet him. Maurice showed his badge, and introduced himself, and explained why he was there.

 The man had a look of surprise on his face. Probably because of Maurice's color. A black lawman was a rarity.

 "Come on in," the man said, "I'll tell ya' what I know, an that ain't a bunch! Just what I saw."

 The Marshal got down, loosened the girth on the horse, and followed the man into the house.

 The man named Bert, told Marshal Allen, that Larry Watson the ranch owner, was noticing cows were missing from the herd on the north plateau. So he decided to go check what was happening. Larry rode out the next morning alone. Bert told Maurice, that he wanted Larry to take some cowhands with him, but Larry said he wouldn't be too long.

 Bert said, around two in the afternoon, he and some men decided to ride to the plateau to see what was taking Larry so long.

 When they got there, Larry was lying on the ground with a black man kneeling over him. All the men pulled out their rifles. Bert said the man hollered out to them, saying he was trying to help Larry, but he was to late too do anything. Bert said there were several cows grouped up nearby, so they figured the man was a rustler.

One of the cow hands shot his rifle at the man over Larry, and the man drew his pistol and shot back at him. All the cowhands horses scattered at the shots fired, and that allowed the man to get on his horse and ride off.

Bert said they took chase, but the black man disappeared, and they could not make out his trail. He just vanished. They rode back, and two men that had stayed with Larry said Larry was dead.. They rode back to town and told Sheriff Davis what had taken place. Davis got with Texas Ranger Will Barrett, and they gathered up a posse to hunt for the killer.

Bert also told Marshal Allen; "One of the cowhands said it was Bryan Joiner, and he had met him in Austin months before. He also warned he was fast and good with a gun. He also told us, he could have killed the man he shot at when they rode up, but he didn't."

"Well do you think he was telling the truth about trying to help your boss?" Marshal Allen asked.

"Marshal I don't know, but there were cattle gathered up, and it looked to us Larry ran up on him, and Bryan Joiner shot him. We figured he was rummaging for money."

"Did anyone check to see if Larry had fired his gun?"

"I don't think so marshal, but we can check, it's hanging in here on the wall."

Bert got up and took the gun in its holster down, and carried it to Maurice. Maurice pulled the pistol out of its holster. Marshal Allen opened the side gate and turned the cylinder.

"Well he put up a fight," Marshal Allen remarked, "five shots were fired. But at who is the question?"

"Marshal, I don't want to sound disrespectful, but it seems to me you are defending this murderer Joiner."

"No sir I am not, but to accuse someone of murder, you have to prove it. No one saw Mr. Joiner do it. The only ones that really know that answer is your boss and Joiner. And your boss is not able to help. So I got to get Mr. Joiner and see if he will talk. If he can't prove any different it will be up to the jury."

Bert nodded his head in agreement.

"If you will excuse me sir, I will be on my way. Thank you for talking to me. I have a lot to do."

"Marshal, you can stay in the bunkhouse if you care to. It's almost empty. Most of the hands are driving over five hundred cattle to a stock yard in Gainesville."

"That will be fine Bert. I can leave early in the morning."

Maurice took his horse to the corral and took his saddle and bridle off. He grabbed a shank of hay, and tossed it over the fence. Bert took him to the bunkhouse. Inside were three men playing cards. Bert introduced Maurice to them, and they all shook his hand in greeting.

The men told the marshal there was some stew and coffee warmed by the fire. Maurice had some stew and coffee. It felt good to have a meal. He rolled a smoke, and sat thinking about Bryan Joiner, and the charges against him. It made him think of so many possible outcomes.

After finishing his smoke, Marshal Allen thanked the men, and laid down on a bunk. It felt comforting. He was sleeping in no time.

Marshal Allen was awake before daylight. He was rested and ready to begin his search for Bryan. He knew this was not going to easy, and he knew Bryan Joiner was expecting someone to be hunting for him.

As he was pulling on his boots, one of the cowhands handed him a cup of coffee. It was dark and strong.

"Thanks friend," Maurice said, "that will hit the spot."

"Glad to share marshal, gonna' have some eats with us?"

"No friend, I gotta' get moving. Have a lot of saddle time coming I'm a figuring. But thanks for asking."

He said goodbye, and stepped out the door. It was a cool morning. Maurice went to the corral to get his horse. Being cool as it was the horse was a little frisky, and wasn't in any hurry to wear a saddle.

The marshal went to the barn and got a hand full of corn in his hat. The big horse couldn't resist that, walking to Maurice to grab a treat.

"I think we are going to get along just fine." Marshal Allen said to the big black. "I'll care for you ole pal."

After saddling up, he rode off in northerly direction. That's the way Joiner was last seen heading. Maurice rode to a high spot as it was getting daylight. He wanted to see if he could see any smoke from a campfire.

He saw two different smoke trails, but they were coming from large camps. Maurice decided to ride down and check them out. He knew Bryan would not build such a large fire, but he may be there. They were most likely good sized

Indian camps.

As he rode into the first camp, a brave alerted the campsite. There were about fifty or so men, women and children in the camp. The women were cooking meals for the morning breakfast. They were a band of Tonkawa's.

Marshal Allen called to them in Apache. He didn't know the Tonkawa's language, but he knew a lot of them spoke Apache. He told them he called on them as a friend, and wanted to speak to some of the elders.

Several came to meet him. He asked if any had seen Bryan, and gave a description of him and his horse. Several raised their hands. Maurice got down off his big horse and one of the braves took hold of the reins. The big horse didn't care for that, and started to rare, swinging his feet.

"Easy big boy," Marshal Allen spoke as he took back the reins, "it's OK boy, easy."

He patted the horse on the chest to calm him down and dropped the reins.

"He'll be OK, just let him stand. He'll not go off." The horse started to eat some grass.

The elders motioned for Maurice to sit, and they gathered with him. One of the men said something in Tonkawa language. Another man told Maurice in Apache, the man said he saw him two days ago, and that he had seen Bryan five days ago.

The other elders all reported seeing Bryan Joiner at different times also. One man said he thought Joiner had taken up with the Comanche's camped about twenty miles northwest from where they are now.

Marshal Allen figured that was the other campfire he saw this morning. Maybe he was in luck of catching up with Bryan faster than he had figured. He would have to move quickly and stealthy, as not to be seen by any Comanche braves.

Maurice thanked the elders for their help. They asked him to have a meal with them. He told him time was of the ascents, and and he had to get along. They gave him some deer meat and bread to take with him. He thanked them for their help and went to get his horse. The horse was not where he left him but was with a couple of the Indians mares. Maurice chuckled.

He started riding northwest. If things went well, he would be at the Comanche camp site in late afternoon. The big black horse moved well on the trail. He was sure-footed and strong paced.

Mid-day he came to a nice clear stream. He decided to stop and have a quick bite of the deer meat, and have some coffee. Maurice gathered some small dried hard wood to make a fire with no smoke. As the fire was warming the coffee, he walked the big horse to the stream for a drink.

The horse was thirsty, and gladly drank of the cold water. Suddenly he raised his head with his ears twitching back and forth, and was staring at something he either saw or sensed. Marshal Allen eased his hand to one of his pistols. The last thing he needed was gun shots. In this clear air the shots would be heard for miles. He stood and waited.

A figure stepped into view. It was a squaw.

"You come for him?" She asked in English.

"For who?" Marshal Allen replied.

"He knows you are coming, Marshal, and he wants no trouble. He did nothing wrong."

"Who are you speaking of?"

"Why are you acting as you know nothing of what I speak?"

Maurice shook his head, and said; "Step over here and let's talk." She nodded her head a started across the stream.

Maurice tied the big black to sapling with a lead rope, and motioned to a log on the stream bank. She sat down.

"OK, are you asking about me coming for Bryan Joiner?"

"You know I am. Don't be so coy Marshal!"

"News travels fast from tribe to tribe,"

Maurice figured some one from the Tonkawa's sent word.

"I take it you have spoken with him." Maurice asked.

"Yes I have Marshal. He told me he was trying to help that cattleman. He was in the area when he heard shots, so he rode to see what was going on. When he got there a gun battle was taking place, and he could see that rustlers had gathered some cattle, and the owner was trying to get them back. He wounded two of the rustlers and they all ran off. When Bryan got to the cattleman he was wounded. It was a bad wound, and he tried to help, but it was to late, he died in his arms."

"Well if that was so," Maurice asked, "why did he shoot at

the ranch hands?"

"Why? They shot at him. He fired back to scatter them so he could get away. He knew they were going to kill him asking no questions. He could have killed several of them, but he didn't want too."

"Why didn't he go to the authorities?"

"He thought of doing that Marshal, but a black man with a dead cattleman, and his cattle, and no bodies to prove his intent. He knew they wouldn't believe him, and he would be hanged."

"Well that's a point to be considered ma'am, but he has to come in and stand trial, and speak his story."

"He won't stand a chance Marshal without any of the rustlers to prove it."

"Well it is my duty as a sworn lawman, I have to take him in."

"He wants no trouble with you Marshal, but he will not let you take him in without proof of his actions."

"Does he know where the rustles have gone?"

"Yes he has been following them. That's how he ended up at our camp. The rustlers traveled passed us. They were seen by one of our braves. The brave said he saw two men wounded in the group."

"Will he talk to me?"

"He wants your help Marshal."

"OK, take me to him."

The woman got up, and told Maurice to follow, as she crossed the stream. Maurice got on his horse and followed. The squaw moved quickly. The trail was clear and very

91

straight. After about an hour the big black horse was twitching his ears and lifting his head. Marshal Allen knew he was being watched. The squaw stopped.

"You wait here Marshal, I will get him."

She trotted down the trail. Maurice got down from his horse, it was nervous. He stroked the big black's and told him it was OK. In about ten minutes, the squaw came back.

"Let me hold your gun belt Marshal, he will then come forward."

"I can't do that!"

"I give you my word, if you do, he means no trouble. If you do not, you will have to do it the hard way."

Maurice thought for a minute. This could be a trap. This goes against all that he believed. The squaw held out her hand.

Maurice unbuckled his belt, and handed it out to her. After all she knew not of his pistol under his shirt. She took the gun belt and hung it on a tree branch about twenty feet away, and turned looking down the trail. A tall well built black man stepped forward.

"Are you Bryan Joiner?" Marshal Allen asked.

"Yes Marshal, I am. I want no trouble, I need to talk to you."

"Let's talk then."

They walked to a downed tree, and sat down. Bryan Joiner started to tell his story.

"I was riding toward Dallas to buy some supplies, and I heard shots being fired. As I came over a rise, I saw a man riding toward five cowhands shooting at him. He was hollering, "Those are my cattle, let loose!" He was shooting back at them, but he took a shot that knocked him off his horse. I drew my gun and charged in. I'm a good shot, but on a running horse it's hard to be accurate. I did hit two of them though, and they turned their horses and rode hard away. Wish I'd a dropped a couple of 'em."

"What happened then?" Marshal Allen asked.

"I got off my horse to check on the wounded man. He was hit hard, and I knew he didn't have much of a chance. He thanked me for trying to help, and passed while I was trying to stop the blood. As I was laying him down, a bunch of cowhands came riding at me. I heard one shout, "He's shot the boss!" At that point they all were shooting. I fired back, not to hit anyone, but to scatter them. It worked and I got on my horse and rode out as fast as I could."

Marshal Allen thought about what he had been told. It wasn't he didn't believe Bryan, but he had no physical proof. He was sworn by law to take Bryan Joiner back for trail. What worried him, was it would come down one mans word against five or six others. It didn't look good.

Another problem was, Bryan wasn't going to be easy to take back. He was now thinking he should have brought some help. What to do?

"Brian, you have yourself between a rock and a wall!" Maurice said. "All you have is your story against theirs."

"I know marshal, that's why I'm tracking them, I have to have a witness."

"Do you know where they are?"

"Yes I do. A Comanche brave followed them. They about five miles north of here resting, and caring for the wounded. They will scat as so as the wounded men are able to travel"

"I'll tell you what I'll do Bryan," Maurice said, "I will help you to try and catch them. But I don't see them giving up easy. They know what's at stake."

"That's what I was hoping marshal, your help."

"I have to tell you this Bryan, I will still have to take you back. When we get back to Dallas, I will stand for you at trial. But if we are able to capture anyone of them, you know they are going to blame you! So it will be my word against them. I say that, because the jury is not going to believe you, and I do not have any physical facts. And if we can't get anyone of them to admit, it's gonna' be rough."

Bryan sat there and just stared at the trees. He turned to Maurice, and told him he was willing to take the chance with him behind him.

Marshal Allen was relieved to hear that. He turned to

Bryan Joiner and said; "Good. Let's get ready to ride son."
Maurice and Bryan walked into the Comanche village to prepare to for the ride to the camp of the rustlers. They checked their guns to be sure they were fully loaded. They did expect a fight. Some of the braves asked if they needed any help. Marshal Allen said it would be helpful, but told them not to shoot to kill. They got what they needed, and started off. They rode slowly not to make much noise.
About hours ride one of the braves held up his hand. He pointed and said in a low voice that the camp was close. They all got off their horse and tied them to brush.
They spread out, and moved quietly. Maurice could hear them talking. He gathered everyone, and told them they would charge in to surprise them, and possibly they would surrender. He hoped.
When all were in place Maurice gave the command with his hand. They charged in. The rustlers were shocked, and caught off guard, but immediately grabbed for their pistols. Shots rang out and it was over in seconds. Not one rustler was left standing. The marshal checked each one. So much for wounding, they all were dead!
Maurice was disappointed. He was hoping for at least one or two to give up when they saw they were so out numbered. But it gave him an idea. He told Bryan to help him load each mans gun with bullets from their gun belts. He them put them in his saddle bags. He told Bryan he thought he had an idea that would save everything.
"If my idea works Bryan, you're off the hook. Keep your fingers crossed."

96

Bryan shook his head, and replied; "Hope your right friend."

Marshal Allen examined the men for identification. Only three could be confirmed. He put their papers in his shirt.

The group got together and buried the dead men. Maurice told the braves to take the rustlers equipment, and horses, back to camp to keep. It was things he knew the tribe could use. They thanked him, for they could really use it.

After getting their things packed at the Comanche camp, Maurice and Bryan started for Dallas. The weather was nice everyday they traveled. The days were warm and the nights were cool. They had one day though, about two days from Dallas, they saw a heavy storm approaching them. Luckily, they found an abandoned adobe structure close by. They quickly repaired the roof as best they could. It wasn't perfect, but would do in a pinch. There was a lean-to behind the adobe. It wasn't great, but would give the horses some protection. They covered the horses backs with their rain slickers to help out.

After a thorough check inside the adobe, they found three rattle snakes.

"Looks like we have dinner Bryan."

"I'll stick with the beans marshal," Bryan replied, "not real hasty bout eaten snakes much."

Maurice shrugged his shoulders, and grinned.

"Shame to miss out pal. They're tasty fried."

"Thanks anyway, marshal."

There was enough wood to cook the meal and warm the adobe overnight. Maurice started a fire to cook, and Bryan stood at the door watching the approaching storm. There was some strong winds, blazing lighting and roaring thunder. The roof had a few leaks, but wasn't to bad. They placed pots to catch what dripped in. At least it wasn't dripping on the bunks.

As Maurice was working on the fire, Bryan fired a shot.

Marshal Allen grabbed his gun thinking was meant for him. Bryan looked at him and said; "If I was gonna do you in marshal, I'd-a done it before this."

On the floor, there was a rabbit. Evidently, it was using the adobe as shelter in bad weather, and ran through the door to to get away from the storm. Maurice took a deep breath, and smiled.

"Sorry Bryan. Just all these years.........!"

"I understand marshal. Don't blame you I'd a done the same. I'll even share."

Wasn't long and dinner was ready. There was a board laying across two flat rocks that made a make shift table. There was also two small barrels to use as seats. They poured coffee, filled their plates, and sat down to eat. Maurice had beans and fried snake, and Bryan had beans and rabbit.

"Want some rabbit marshal?"

"I know you can eat the whole rabbit, I have plenty. Thanks though."

As they were finishing the meal, and drinking coffee, Bryan asked Marshal Allen what he had in mind to help get him cleared.

"All I can say right now Bryan, is I am sure I can prove you did not kill that rancher if I can get some finishing touches to what I have now. I just need one more item, and I am praying it is not lost."

"And if it is lost marshal............What then?"

"Let's put it this way Bryan. If I can't come up with what I need it is gonna' be tough."

"Well marshal, I'm not so sure of taking that risk."

"If you run Bryan, you're done for sure. You will never get a chance, they will hang you on the spot."

Bryan stared at his cup, and shook his head. He had to make a choice. Run or trust Marshal Allen.

Much wasn't said after that. They cleaned up from the meal, and got ready for bed. Maurice put some wood on the fire for the night, and they both got on a bunk. The storm carried through the night.

In the morning, Maurice had the coffee on. He glanced at the bunk Bryan had used, and it was empty. This worried him. He walked to the door and could see foot prints leading around to the back of the adobe. He followed them.

"Lookin' for me?"

"No Bryan, just checking on the horses, but I see you already did. Coffee will be ready in a couple of minutes."

Maurice took a deep breathe, and walked back inside. Marshal Allen rolled a smoke, and sipped his coffee. Bryan sipped his coffee, and stared out the door. It was a clear day, cooled down some from the rain.

"Someone's coming!" Bryan said callously. They both cleared their jackets off their pistols.

A man, showing his age some, rode up to the adobe, and swung down from his saddle walked to the door.

"See ya found the place." He said. "I didn't have time to get here, the rain came on me fast."

"You must have gottin' soaked." Maurice said to him.

"Not to much, got under a rock overhang. It was OK except when the wind would blow my way. Got damp some though. Got some coffee?"

The Marshal pointed to the pot, looked at Bryan, and raised his eyebrows. Bryan just shrugged his shoulders.

The man poured a cup full and sat on a wood box he pulled from under a bunk.

"You from around this way much?" Marshal Allen asked.

"You might just say that, I was born in this house, my friend. I was a comin' to fix her up and sit a spell."

"Born here, I never would have thought I'd meet the owner." Maurice told him.

"Been a while since my last stay. Thought I'd settle for a while, and fix it up some."

"You built it?" Bryan asked.

"No, my Dad, who was a Mex, and my Ma, a Squaw, put her together."

"So you just moved on to better pasture?"

"No, we was attacked by Injuns. They kilt Ma an Pa, an took me. I was about ten then, I 'spose."

"Live with them long?" Maurice asked.

"Bout five, six years. Saw a wagon train go by one day,

103

and snuck off after them that night."

"That was an experience to remember, I spent many years with several Indian tribes, myself." Maurice replied.

"Ya' it was, but I wanted to get where people lived in a town or ranch, and worked together. When some found out I was a mix breed, they turned their nose at me, but some were nice too!"

"Well it was nice to meet you friend," Maurice told him, "we gotta get a move on. Headin' for Dallas."

"You that Black Marshal?" The man asked.

"As a matter of fact, I am. How'd you know?"

"Heard a lot bout ya. You ever catch up with that cattle rustler?"

"No, I never did. He just disappeared."

"Everyone's a thinking you would get 'em."

"Well can't get 'em all, my friend. Hope all goes well for you, my friend. Thanks for the hospitality."

They got their things together, and went out to saddle up. The man waved as they went out.

"Why did you tell him that?" Bryan asked.

"Just playing it safe Pal. Don't want to get ambushed."

They rode on to Dallas. The rain had cooled it off some but that didn't last. It was cool at night but was getting hot and humid during the day. There was plenty of game along the trail, and some different fruits, and veggies, to make some good meals.

When getting just outside of Dallas, Maurice asked Bryan to lay back so he could ride into town and tell the sheriff what was taking place. He was also afraid if he brought

Bryan into town they would string him up immediately.
Marshal Allen rode into Dallas so he could get to the
sheriffs office without being seen. He rode up to the
sheriffs from around the back of the building. He
dismounted and walked to the back door. He knocked.
Sheriff Bert Davis came to see who was knocking. He was
puzzled, and asked who was there before opening the door.
Maurice answered, and Bert opened the door.

"What ya' coming around back for Marshal?" He asked.

"I'll explain inside Sheriff!" Maurice said. "Got a lot to tell
ya'." Bert motioned him in, and pulled the door behind him.
When they sat down, Maurice started telling the sheriff of
what he had found, and what he had in mind.

"Did you get him?" Bert asked.

"Yes, sheriff, but there is so much involved."

Maurice told Bert what had taken place, and told Bert he
thought Bryan was innocent, and had a plan to prove it. He
told Bert he would bring Bryan Joiner in after dark. But let
no one know he was in the jail.

Marshal Allen told the sheriff to get a hold of a judge to set
up a trial. He also said, to have the judge pick the jury with
no cattlemen among them. He also asked the sheriff to get
with the doctor or mortician, and see if they had removed
the bullet that had killed rancher Larry Watson. He told
Bert that was very important. Bert said it was a going to
take some time.

"Sheriff, I need you to get all this together as quickly as we
can. And we can't let anyone know, Bryan Joiner is here,
until just before the trial takes place. If the cattlemen know

he's in this jail, they will come for him."

"Good point Marshal. I'll make sure everyone knows to keep their mouth shut. Just hope you know what you're doing. I'll get busy." Bert put his hat on, and gave Maurice the key to the back door as he walked out.

Marshal Allen locked the door behind Bert, and went out the back door.

Marshal Allen rode out, and met with Bryan. He told
Bryan he had met with the sheriff, and that he had his plan
in action. He said he was taking to the sheriffs office after it
got dark.

"I've got my trust in you Marshal. I hope it all comes
together."

"I'm doing all I can young fella'." Maurice said, as he
patted Bryan on the back.

As it got dark they started to ride into town, making sure to
keep out of sight using the back streets. They didn't run into
many people. When they did, they kept their hats low and
just waved.

They rode to the back of the sheriffs office, tied their
horses, and went in the back door. Maurice pulled the
curtains, and lit a lantern. He doubled checked to make sure
the front door was still locked, and started making coffee.

After some snooping, he found a bottle of whiskey and
poured two glasses. He was hoping Sheriff Davis would be
coming with some news. He could tell Bryan was a little
nervous. When the coffee was ready, he filled two cups.
They both sat down, neither saying much. Both of them
where getting hungry also.

Somebody was fooling with the door. Marshal Allen told
Bryan to duck into the jail room and made sure his guns
clear. The door opened, it was Sheriff Davis, he was
carrying a bag.

"Well I got done more than I thought I would. The judge

was home, and he understands what you are trying to do. He is going around tomorrow and try to find ten people that are not from around here. That way they wont have a negative opinion. He told me he had to appoint an attorney to stand for the rancher. He also told me you need to get one to defend Mr. Joiner."

"I'll do that Sheriff." Maurice answered.

"You a lawyer too?" Bert asked.

"No I'm not, but I'm sure I can handle this case if I have the evidence I need."

"Some of these lawyers are pretty sneaky." Bert replied. "I've seen 'em get some crooked men set free. OK, here's some eats for ya. Thought you'd be hungry." He reached into the bag and brought out two wrapped items. Marshal Allen thanked him.

"Wheres your man?" Bert asked.

"Right here Sheriff." Bryan said as he stepped into the room. "Well young man," Bert replied, "better take that gun belt off, and eat." Marshal Allen nodded at Bryan, and he dropped his belt.

Bert had gotten two roast beef sandwiches on a roll. He told them; "Told her I had two drunks locked up and had to feed 'em. Ya owe me a dollar."

"Gladly Sheriff, here ya go." Maurice said, and put a dollar on the desk.

After finishing their sandwiches, they had another coffee. Sheriff Davis told Bryan he had to sleep in the jail cell for the night, and Bryan didn't like that very much, and let it be known.

"Look young man, I and the Marshal are really sticking our necks out for you, and if those cattlemen know you're here, they'll be a comin' for ya. That is the safest place for you right now." Maurice agreed, and told Bryan it was best.

"I'll even let you take your gun, just in case of trouble." Bert added. That made Bryan feel better.

"Oh, I got something for you." Bert said reaching into the bag. He dropped it on the desk. "This is the bullet from Larry Watson's body. Got it from the undertaker. He said he normally didn't do that but just had a strange feeling bout it." Marshal Allen picked it up and smiled.

"Sheriff, I can't thank you enough. You did great."

"Did what I could Marshal. That's all."

Marshal Allen was so glad he got that one special item. It was what he needed to prove his point.

They sat around for a while talking, and then went on to bed. Bryan went to a jail cell, and Bert locked it. Maurice went to another cell, and laid on a bunk, Bert had a cot he set up. They were snoring in no time.

The next morning, Maurice had the coffee started. Sheriff Davis went to get some breakfast for them. He wasn't gone for long and came back with biscuits and sausage gravy. That hit the spot.

While they were eating, there was a knock on the door. Bert checked to see who it was. He opened the door and said; "Mornin' Judge, come in. Want some coffee?"

"Thanks Sheriff, I will."

"Men, I want you to meet Judge Seeley!"

Maurice, and Bryan stood.

"Sit friends. Finish your breakfast." The judge said, got a cup of coffee, and pulled up a chair to the desk.

Judge Mike Seeley was a good judge. He held to the letter of the law, and was fair. He didn't stand for any shenanigans or tom foolery in his courtroom.

"Marshall Allen, I understand you have some interest in this serious case." Judge Seeley said. "This is a case of possible murder charges. Are you aware of that?"

"Yes Judge I am, but I am sure I can prove the man is innocent."

"Do you have a lawyer to defend the man?"

"No sir, I am going to do it myself."

"Do you have any experience in practicing law?"

"No sir I don't, but if my evidence turns out, I do not need any."

"I hope you're right. If not, the lawyer for the cattlemen will tear you to pieces."

"Have you appointed a lawyer for the cattlemen yet?"
Sheriff Davis asked the judge.

"Yes I have." The judge replied. "He's new around here.
He comes from Boston. He has a good reputation and has
handled some big cases. He has a fine record."I've looked
at his papers. His name is James Glass."

Maurice was surprised. Was that the man who joined them
along their way to Dallas, a few weeks back? He didn't
seem like a lawyer. He was more like drifter.

"Is the prisoner under good guards?" The judge asked.

"Yes sir he is." Marshal Allen answered, as he nodded
toward Bryan Joiner. The judge's mouth dropped.

"Shouldn't he be in a cell?"

"I trust him, and I believe he is truly innocent." Judge
Seeley's eyebrows went up.

Maurice told Judge Seeley what he had learned and told
him Bryan's side of the story, and how he tried to catch up
with rustlers to prove his innocence.

Judge Seeley asked if they caught up with them. Maurice
told him they did, but they wouldn't give up, and went
down in the attempt to take them in.

"At that, I'd say you don't have a chance in hell." The
judge said. "The man has nothing to back up his claims,
and that lawyer is gonna sink your boat, marshal."

Maurice stood up and asked the judge to step to the back
room with him. When they got there, Marshal Allen
reached Into his pocket, and placed the bullet in the judge's
hand.

"Sir, this bullet, and you are going to prove them all

113

wrong."

"I don't understand!" Judge Seeley said.

"Just leave it to me Sir. I got this figured out! At least I sure hope so."

Judge Seeley just shook his head, and said; "Hope your right!"

They walked back to the front office, and the Judge told them court would open at the town hall at noon the next day. He also told them, he would have the cattlemen informed in the morning, so it wouldn't give time enough to cause trouble. He wished all a good day, and walked out.

"Jim Glass," Bryan said, "wasn't that the guy that rode with you and your friend?"

"Yes, I believe so, same name. He didn't seem like a lawyer. Thought he was just a drifter, or a cowhand."

Sheriff Davis told them he was going to get food for the rest of the day. He asked Maurice to lock the door as he stepped out.

The next morning, Judge Seeley, came to see Sheriff Davis. He told him to bring the marshal and Bryan Joiner to town hall before noon. He also told him to come in the back way so that would be less chance of trouble.

Maurice, Bryan and Sheriff Davis had coffee and bacon biscuits for breakfast. Sheriff Davis told the marshal, he would go in the front door, and for Bryan and him to come in the back as Judge Seeley suggested.

At eleven thirty, they started for town hall. The Marshal and Bryan went out the back door. Marshal Allen was nervous. He was hoping there would be no one waiting to ambush them. He pulled his jacket back to have his two Colt pistols clear. He had his saddle bags over his shoulder.

Because of the news of the trial the main street to the town hall was fairly crowded, with no one on the back streets. They moved quickly.

As Sheriff Davis was approaching town hall, a group of cowhand from the Watson ranch rode up to him.

"Where's your prisoner Sheriff?" Frank Wingo the ranch trail boss asked.

"Don't worry Frank, he's safe."

"Is he in the jail?"

"I said he is safe, and gonna' stay that way Frank."

Frank turned and told one of the men to check the jail.

"Frank! I want no trouble. I told you he was safe, and he's gonna' stay that way." Sheriff Davis told Frank. "Now stand down and wait for the trial, or I'll arrest you for interfering in the due process of the law."

"We already had a trial sheriff, weeks ago." Frank said.

"There will be no lynching as long as I am the Dallas sheriff, Frank. Now stand back or I will bar you from entering."

Frank started to draw for his pistol, but Bert out drew him. Frank froze in his saddle.

"Who wants to go down after I shoot Frank?" Bert said. No one moved.

"OK then men, drop your guns at the door when you enter." Sheriff Davis ordered. They all got down and walked toward the entrance grumbling to each other. Bert was relieved.

Marshal Allen and Bryan came in the back door, and Judge Seeley was sitting at a desk writing some notes.

"Have a seat men," he said, "we'll be getting started in just a few minutes. I'll have you called in when I'm ready."

The court room was filling fast. Frank Wingo asked Sheriff Davis if he and his men were going to be on the jury.

"Judge Seeley has already picked the jury Frank. Just sit down."

Franks face turned red, and he replied; "What type of trial is this?"

"A fair one Frank."

"Sounds to me like it's rigged." Frank answered.

A lot of the men in the room were agreeing with Frank. The sheriff told them to sit, and quiet down. He then walked to the judges door and opened it.

"We're ready judge." he said.

Judge Seeley stepped into the courtroom.

"Hear ye, hear ye." Bert called out. "All rise."

Judge Seeley entered, sat at his table and tapped his gavel, saying; "This court will come to order, all be seated."

Judge Seeley asked the jury to be seated, and asked Sheriff Bert Davis to bring the defendant and his council. Bert opened the door to the judge's chamber, and motioned the marshal and Bryan to come in. He pointed to a table and two chairs where they were to sit.

"Bryan Joiner." Judge Seeley said. "Please step forward."

Bryan walked up to the judge's bench.

"Bryan Joiner, you are charged with cattle rustling, and murder." The judge said. "How do you plead to these charges?"

"Not guilty sir." That caused the crowd stir some. "Do you have council?"

"Yes sir I do." Bryan answered, pointing to Marshal Allen.

"You may return to your seat, and I will have the attorney representing the Watson ranch, give his opening statements." Bryan turned and sat down, looking at the marshal. Marshal Allen patted him on his leg.

James Glass stepped forward. He glanced around the court room. He looked at the jury, and nodded his head. He then looked out toward the crown of seated people, and waved his hand at them. He then turned and looked at Maurice.

"Good to see you again, my friend. I'll make this as short as I can." The marshal nodded his head to him.

118

"Gentlemen of the jury! What we have here is an out and out case of rustling, and the killing of fine Texas citizen. Larry Watson, a member of your community, and a fine Texas rancher. He was killed in in cold blood." James Glass told them. "Mr Joiner, sitting over there, got caught stealing cattle belonging to Mr. Watson, and Mr. Joiner killed him."

"Judge, isn't he swaying the jury?"

"He is making his opening statement marshal. Continue Mr. Glass."

"Thank you sir." Jim Glass replied. "Gentlemen of the jury. Mr. Joiner was going through Mr. Watson's pockets when five riders from his ranch rode up. They had heard the gunfire and came to investigate. "

"That's not so judge, I was trying to help him!" Bryan stood and cried out.

"Sit down Mr. Joiner! You will have your chance to tell your side." Judge Seeley said. Bryan sat down shaking his head.

"Are any of the five men that rode up on the scene here?" Attorney Glass asked. Five men stood up. Glass pointed to one of them, and asked him to take a seat next to the judge's bench. The man walked to the bench, but before he could sit, Sheriff Davis stepped up with a bible in his hand.

"Put your hand on the bible and swear to tell the truth, and nothing but the truth, so help you God."

"I do."

Jim glass walked to him and asked: "Your name sir?"

"Bertram Wells."

"What do you do at the ranch Mr. Wells?"

"I am the ranch manager. I took care of Mr. Watson's affairs."

"Did you see Mr. Joiner at the scene?"

"Yes sir, I did."

"Did you see anyone else there?"

"No, he was alone."

"And what was Mr. Joiner doing?"

"Looked like he was going through his pockets."

Bryan Joiner stood up, but the marshal pulled on his pant leg to sit back down.

"What happened then?"

"He shot at us and we scattered."

"Anyone hit in your group?"

"No sir."

"And then what happened?"

"When we gathered up, the rustler was gone."

"You may sit back to your seat. Thank you." Jim Glass said. "Your honor, I am finished. I think the court has heard all."

"Do you want to question Mr Joiner?"

"No your honor. He is not going to say anything that can be of any help to his cause."

The judge asked Marshal Allen if he wanted Mr. Joiner to testify? Maurice stood, and asked Bryan to take the witness seat. Sheriff Davis had Bryan place his hand on the bible, and asked him the same as he did to Mr. Wells. Bryan sat down. The marshal walked to him.

121

"Mr. Joiner, you have heard the charges against you, and the testimony of the witness. What do you have to say?"

"I heard some shooting and rode up to see what was going on." Bryan told him. "When I got there, there were five men shooting at the rancher, who was on the ground. So I charged in shooting at the rustlers."

"What happened then, Mr. Joiner?"

"I hit two of them, and they scattered off. I wished I could have downed one of them, but shooting from a running horse isn't the best."

"So you did chase them away?"

"Yes, I did. But I would have liked to had knocked one down to prove my actions."

"Were you going through Mr. Watson's pockets?"

"No I was trying to help him. He thanked me, and then he passed away. It was a bad wound, I couldn't do anything for him."

"What happened when Mr. Watson's men rode up?"

"They all had guns in their hands, so I fired at them to make them scatter. I knew they would hang me to the nearest tree."

"Did you hit any of them?"

"No. I didn't want to make matters worse. I could have killed any one of them, but I just wanted to make them scatter, so I could get away."

"Did they scatter?"

"Yes, and it gave me a chance to get on my horse and make a run for it."

"Where were you going to go?"

"I followed the trail of the five rustlers hoping to catch up with them."

"What were you going to do if you did?"

"I was hoping to take one captive to prove my innocence."

"Your honor, this man is trying to make us believe he was trying to help Mr. Watson, and has no proof he was not alone." Jim Glass objected.

"Let the defense finish Mr. Glass!"

"He is trying to pull at the hearts of the jury, your honor!"

"Sit down Mr. Glass!" He sat down.

"Your honor," Marshal Allen said, "I was given the job of tracking down Mr. Joiner, and bring him to justice. When I caught up with him, he told me his story, and he was on the trail of the five men that had attacked Mr. Watson. We tried to capture the five men, but they went down in a gun battle."

"There you have it your honor. There is no proof!" Jim Glass called out.

"Mr. Glass!..... If you disrupt this court, one more time, I will have you removed." Judge Seeley told him.

"Your honor, Mr. Joiner has no proof, but I think I have."

"What do you have marshal?"

"I will need a barrel of water brought in, and a lid for it, your honor."

"What?" The judge asked.

"I know it is a strange request judge, but that's what I need, and your help."

Judge Seeley was puzzled, but asked Sheriff Davis to see what he could find.

Bert went out with six men and came back with a barrel, and the men were carrying buckets of water to fill it. They set it on the floor, and poured the water in it.

"Your honor. I have the bullet that was taken from Mr. Watson's body." Maurice put it on the judge's bench. "I want you to look at this bullet very closely with this magnifying glass."

The judge looked at the bullet, and back at the Marshal.

"Your honor, every guns rifling leaves distinct marks from its barrel. Everyone is different. In my saddle bags, I have the guns from the five men we took down in the gun fight. I have Mr. Joiner's gun also."

"What do plan to do, Marshal Allen."

"I am going to fire each gun and have you examine the bullets."

"That is ridicules judge!" Jim Glass spoke out. "How can that possibly prove anything?"

"Mr. Glass, I have warned you, and this is your last warning. Now sit, and shut up." Judge Seeley said, and slammed his gavel on his bench. Jim sat down.

Marshal Allen pulled a pistol from his saddlebag.

"This is Mr. Joiners gun, your honer."

He pointed it into the barrel, cocked it, and placed the lid over it. When he pulled the trigger, the blast was muffled. Some water sprayed from the small gap, hitting the marshal.

Maurice reached into the barrel, and retrieved the spent bullet, handing it to Judge Seeley.

Judge Seeley inspected the bullet, and compared it to the one from Mr. Watson's body.

"Marshal, the bullet from Mr. Joiner's gun, is not the same type of bullet, and the rifle marks do not match."

Jim Glass stood up, judge Seeley looked at him, and Jim quickly sat back down.

"Then it is not possible that Mr. Joiner's gun killed Mr. Watson!" Marshal Allen said.

"Your honor. May I approach the bench?" Jim Glass asked.

The judge motioned Jim to the bench.

"Your honor, the bullets could have been changed."

"Even if so Mr. Glass, the marks do not match, and the bullet is not of the same caliber." Jim Glass's face went blank, and he returned to his seat.

Marshal Allen pulled another pistol from his bags, and fired it, getting wetter. He handed it to Judge Seeley. He compared it, and shook his head. No match.

The marshal pulled another pistol, and fired it. No match! The third pistol was fired, and the bullet handed to the judge. He carefully examined it and compared it side by side to the bullet in question.

"Marshal, we have a match!"

Marshal Allen looked at the tag on the pistol, and said; "Judge, this gun belonged to Will Anderson. He was the killer of Mr. Watson."

The crowd stated talking among themselves in excitement.

"I know of him!" One man called out. "He's been a rustling for years, but never caught. Was with Clint Berger's bunch!"

"I have his pistol tagged too, your honor." Maurice added. Jim Glass got up and shook Maurice's hand, telling him he did a fine job.

"Hope to have a drink with you marshal! I lost my first case against you!" Jim told him. He tipped his hand to Judge Seeley, and walked out.

Judge Seeley asked the jury if they had anything to say, and they all agreed Bryan was not guilty as charged. The judge slammed his gavel on the bench, and hollered; "Case dismissed, court adjourned!"

Bryan gave Maurice a great hug, and thanked him.

"You saved my life marshal, and cleared my name."

"Glad I could help Bryan, so glad I could."

Sheriff Bert Davis came to them and gave his congratulations to them both.

"That was quite a job you did solving that case marshal. I wouldn't have figured that out. Never heard of it being done before."

"I read one time how each gun has its own markings from the rifling in the bore. That's why I collected and tagged them."

Bertram Wells came over, and shook the marshals hand, and then said to Bryan Joiner: "Mr. Joiner, I want to thank you for trying to help my boss. I'm sorry this happened to you, but when we rode up, it didn't look good. I am so sorry, and I'm glad you were cleared. The marshal did a fine job!"

"Marshal, Bryan, let's have a drink to celebrate." Sheriff Davis suggested.

"Sounds good to me sheriff." Maurice replied.

"Sure does sheriff." Bryan added, with a big smile on his face.

"Mind if I join you?" Judge Seeley added.

"Come on, the more the merrier." Bert said.

Bert, Maurice, Bryan and the judge went down the street, to the Raging Bull Saloon.

They walked up to the bar, and the bartender wiped the bar. For a moment the room went silent, then there was a lot of murmuring among the crowd.

"What ya having men?"

"I think we all would like a glass of your top bourbon." Sheriff Davis replied.

"That round is on me!" A voice called out. It was Jim Glass. The bartender nodded, and started pouring into the glasses.

"That was a hellava' show you put on today, marshal."

"I just had the proof Jim. That's all."

"Well you had your head on your shoulders when figured it out." Jim told Maurice, and put his money on the bar.

"I've been up against some good men in court, and never lost a case, but I did today."

"I'm sure it didn't ruin your reputation Jim."

"No, but it had my tail between my legs."

The marshal tipped his glass at him, and took a draw from his glass. Just as he did the bat wing doors flew open, and Frank Wingo stepped in, and looked at the bar.

"Some pretty fancy trickery in court today." He said. "Set up jury, made up story, and a paid off judge."

"It was all legal fella'." Jim Glass told him.

"You know your self it was crooked." Frank answered. "You laid out the facts, and they over ruled you."

"No fella' they didn't. The marshal had the proof, and the murder weapon. Even the name of the man who killed your boss. One of the men in the courtroom even knew of that man's reputation."

"Well I ain't buying it. I'm gonna settle it here and now."

"Don't even try to grab for your gun." A voice from behind Frank said. It was Bertram Wells the ranch boss. Frank turned his head to look at him. Bertram Wells was holding a gun on him.

"Why you........" Frank said, and grabbed for Bertram's pistol. There was a loud pow! Frank dropped to his knees, and fell over. He was dead. Bertram Wells put his pistol back in its holster, and walked off.

The sheriff, Bryan, Maurice, Jim and the judge stood there with a look of shock on their face's.

"Marshal Allen," Bryan said, "I think I'm gonna get out of Dallas. I mean far away. There's more than him in this town that still thinks I killed that rancher."

"After what Mr. Wells just did, I think you are going to be OK if you stay. In fact, Mr. Wells will probably hire you if your looking for work. And it will give you a chance to straighten your life."

Bryan nodded his head. The others all agreed with what Marshal Allen had said.

The next morning Maurice saddled up the big black and started back to Kansas. Bryan rode out to the Watson ranch to see about a job.

What gave me to idea to write this story was an article I saw on Wikipedia about a lawman named Bass Reeves. Bass Reeves became the first black marshal west of the Mississippi. It is said he was the real Lone Ranger.

He rode a white horse. Wore two ivory handled Colt revolvers. He stood 6'2". He wore a black hat, black coat and gave out silver coins to children.

He arrested over 3000 criminals, and was never wounded in any of the many gun fights he was in. They say he was so tough, he could spit on a brick and break it. They called him "The Indomitable Marshal."

Read his story on Wikipedia!

Made in the USA
Columbia, SC
22 November 2022

71559249R00074